Two for Tripping

A ONE NIGHT STAND COLLEGE HOCKEY ROMANCE

LASAIRIONA MCMASTER

DRAMA LLAMA PUBLISHING

Dedication

For anyone who has ever been touched when they didn't want it...
Sometimes you just need to know you're not alone. Whatever you went through, you didn't deserve it. It wasn't your fault. You deserved to be safe.
We survivors need to hear that from time to time – regardless of how much healing we have done.
You are stronger than you'll ever know.

CHAPTER 1
Quinn

The vibrations rattled through the stage under her feet and into her muscles as Quinn belted out one of her karaoke faves: *I Still Haven't Found What I'm Looking For*. Sure, she was no Bono, but the lyrics shifted something in her every time she sang them.

If there was a time in his life when even the legendary Irish singer Bono didn't know what the hell he was doing, she wasn't going to hold it against herself that she still hadn't found what she was looking for either.

Or she'd at least try. Things like that were easier in theory than practice.

Clutching the microphone with both hands, her gaze skimmed the bar. She didn't need the lyrics on the screen, not for U2, not for Heart, Alannah, Madonna, Roxette, or Stevie. She sang them all with reckless abandon.

Tuesday nights were only ever busy in Pucks because of karaoke. And, while the place wasn't exactly booming, she had a modest audience of drunken freshmen who sang along with her. One guy even held up an unlit lighter, swaying in his chair while yelling that he loved her and wanted her to have his babies.

Flattering though he was, she didn't date younger men. In fact, she hadn't dated anyone in a long time, something she thought might change with each passing Tuesday. Surely she'd find *someone* compatible at some point, right?

If Clary Fairchild managed to find Jace, Alec, and Izzy all at the same time outside a bar in the very first episode of Shadowhunters, there had to be some point in time where Quinn would meet a regular guy.

She didn't even need for him to be a hot Shadowhunter kicking demon ass on the regular, just an everyday guy who wasn't a douchebag. She wasn't asking for much. At least, she didn't think so.

Just someone who perhaps enjoyed karaoke, sci-fi, an occasional game of Mario Kart, and who could carry a conversation beyond 'nice tits' and sending dick pics so she knew what he was equipped with and where he wanted to put it.

Why did guys think dick pics were hot?

Jen the bartender held up a glass, offering a refill when she made eye contact and Quinn nodded. She'd been singing Tuesday night karaoke in Pucks for just over a year, and as she stared down her sophomore year at the University of Minnesota, she knew that wouldn't change any time soon. It was her happy place.

Two women sat at the end of the bar drinking pink cocktails from tall glasses with orange slices hanging on the rims. They made come-to-bed eyes at a guy slouched over a half full glass of something golden. If there had been ice cubes in the tumbler in front of him, they'd long since melted.

His hair was mussed from running his fingers through it, and the collar of his shirt was open and tugged to the side. He turned toward the two chatting women, giving Quinn a perfect line of sight to his face. Frozen in place, goosebumps crept along her skin.

William Morrison. Will. Team captain of the Minnesota Snow Pirates. Former captain. 5 feet 11 inches, 180lbs, right handed shot on the ice, birthday July 6th. And the deliciously hot guy who all but made her forget her damn name when they'd met at Cleo's first book signing. He'd bought her books, like some kind of fictitious too-good-to-be-true man that only exists in women's fantasies – and romance novels. Then she'd lost the receipt with his number on it, and never seen nor heard from him again.

Yup. She'd absolutely – and shamelessly – memorized his stats from the team website. She'd also memorized the curve of his jaw and the precise shade of his cognac brown eyes. She'd crushed on him, hard, but considering she hadn't heard from him and he'd just graduated, she figured that ship had sailed.

Yet there he was, leaning on the bar in front of her, the weight of the world pressing his shoulders forward. His heavy presence almost had her stumbling over her lyrics as she belted out the final few lines of the song. Who was the shell of a man in front of her? And where was the geeky, awkward, smiling team captain she'd met in the bookstore?

She placed the microphone back in the stand and curtseyed to her adoring fans before stepping off the stage.

The two women had moved onto their next drink, chatting back and forth with animated hands and hushed whispers. Their cursory glances at Will suggested one of them was winding up to shoot their shot with him.

Deciding to save them both from potential embarrassment, or worse, ire from Will whose fuck-off vibes were so loud she couldn't fathom how the women hadn't picked up on them, she sidled up to him. She bumped her shoulder against his before sliding onto the empty stool next to him.

"So… what's a guy like you doing in a dive bar like this?"

A small smile tugged at the corner of his mouth. Under his eyes were dark circles, and the bags and red lines behind his heavy eyelids suggested he hadn't slept well for a while. She wanted to hug him.

"And where is your posse? Isn't it a well-known fact that hockey players travel in packs?"

"Hey."

It wasn't a 'fuck off,' but it wasn't a chatty Cathy answer either. She'd take it.

She hooked a thumb at her chest. "Quinn. I mean, hey. I'm Quinn. We met at Cleo's book signing a while back."

When he canted his head an inch and narrowed his gaze, she nodded and took it as an invitation to continue. She had nowhere to go but to his recent success. "Big fan. Congrats on the championship by the way. It must have been a huge deal for you to leave on such a high note. I know it totally sounds like an excuse, but I lost the receipt with your number on it."

The more he stared, the more her cheeks sizzled. Did she have something on her face? Was there something stuck in her hair? She reached up to pat down her wayward auburn waves, unable to stop the word vomit bubbling in the back of her throat.

"Anyway. You were about to have company." She gestured to the two women behind her. "And I... eh... you don't really seem to be in the mood for company, so I... uh..."

"Thought you'd join me instead?" His eyes dropped back to the half-empty glass in front of him.

"Yeah. I thought I'd save you." She winked. "You can thank me later."

Behind the pain and sadness in his brown eyes, his sparkle was nowhere to be seen.

"We can just sit for a little bit."

He nodded but didn't answer. Jen placed Quinn's gin and Sprite on the bar in front of her and accepted her credit card.

"Wanna keep a tab open?"

Quinn nodded and swirled her straw around the slice of lime in her highball glass. "Thanks, Jen."

Jen widened her eyes and jerked her head at Will before mouthing, 'get it girl.'

His eyes drifted to the left of the bar, fixating on something she couldn't see as she ached to fill the silence expanding between them.

On stage, someone with all the audacity in the world butchered *Love Shack* by the B-52's. Had they no respect for the classics? She cringed at the shrieking.

She shook her head and sipped her drink, ignoring the glares from her now-nemeses across the bar. She wasn't normally someone to cock-block another woman, but the sadness seeping from Will's every pore had driven her to act.

If she had to dole out a case of blue balls to a member of her gender to spare Will from even a second more of pain and discomfort, she'd take one for the team.

"I haven't seen you since the book signing." Neutral territory. It wasn't quite 'Let me count the ways,' but she didn't want to spook him.

He didn't tear his eyes from whatever was holding him captive next to the bar, but he nodded and took a drink. "Things have been..." He rotated his wrist, swirling the golden liquid around in the glass. "Crazy."

"I get that. Graduation, am I right?" She took a drink. "I mean, not that I'd know yet, obviously." She cringed again. What the hell was wrong with her? She was a conversational queen, she could make friends out of strangers, but the reserved hockey hottie was apparently her kryptonite.

She swallowed and tried again. "I was starting to feel like I'd dreamt you up like one of my book boyfriends." She snorted, coughed to cover her snort, and choked on the fizzy Sprite that had somehow made its way up her nose.

His lips twitched, but his line of sight was still off to the side of the bar. A picture of Gordie Howe hung on the wall, and the more she stared at it, the more she realized it was crooked. Was that what had been holding his attention?

She tried to avert her gaze, but once she'd seen it, it was all she could see. How could he just sit there, knowing it was crooked and not get up to fix it?

Slipping off the stool next to him, she circled the bar and righted the picture. "That straight?"

Over her shoulder he nodded through a small smile. "A hair more and you're good."

It wasn't much, but she'd take it. She slid the picture frame a tiny bit further before seeking reassurance from him.

"Perfect."

She settled back onto the chair next to him and signaled another round to Jen, who stuck her tongue out and winked before throwing a double thumbs up. Quinn rolled her eyes.

"You sounded great." He gestured up at the stage. "Perfect song choice."

"U2 fan?"

He shook his head. "A fan of any song that doesn't make me feel like an epic fuck up for not having my shit together beyond college graduation."

Wow. Not so reserved after all. "I'll drink to that." She clinked her fresh glass against his.

His eyebrow quirked like he was surprised at her answer.

"There's no rulebook for adulting, William. We all just gotta fuck around and find out."

Wrinkles appeared on his forehead. "Did you just call me William?"

She hiccupped a gasp. "Shit. I guess I did. Sorry. I didn't even think. It just came out."

He picked up his fresh glass, and drained half of it in one go. "I like it."

When his eyes met hers it swallowed the short distance between them. Something warm swam with his sadness, something that sparked in her chest.

His fingertips, cold from cradling the glass, brushed along the curve of her jaw as her eyes fluttered closed. Palm cupping her cheek, his fingers weaved into the loose strands of hair falling around her face.

After a moment, neither of them had moved, so she opened her eyes again to find him studying her.

As she opened her mouth to ask him what he was doing, his lips crashed against hers. He tasted of whisky and his lips were cold from his drink. He smelled of apple and cedarwood, a dizzying, warm, comforting aroma that curled around her.

She gripped his shoulder and his kiss grew more urgent, his tongue spearing at the seam of her lips, demanding entry. When she parted them on a sigh, he invaded, sweeping his tongue against hers and cradling the side of her face in his other hand.

One of the women behind her muttered "bitch," Jen hissed out a "yesssssss," and if Quinn's eyes had been open she probably would have noted a monumental fist pump from her bartending friend.

She couldn't wrap her arms around his neck, but instead layered her hand over his, still on her cheek. She stroked his fingers with her thumb as he kissed her until she was breathless. She tasted a lifetime together, a future, the same connection she'd been hit with at the bookstore when they'd first met. The same tingle that started at the tips of her fingers and traveled all the way to the base of her spine. It scared the fuck out of her.

Dropping his forehead against hers, he sighed, not letting go of her cheek. Her heart swung like Miley Cyrus on her freakin' wrecking ball. What the hell was that?

They sat in silence for a moment, or perhaps twenty, foreheads together, his warm hands holding her face, and her chest rising with startling calmness considering the crazy dance her heart was doing.

Dropping a kiss on her nose, he finally spoke. "Ask me anything." He leaned back and reached for his drink.

She smirked. "Anything?"

He shrugged.

"Okay, favorite TV series."

"The West Wing." There wasn't a beat of hesitation before he answered.

Be still her quickening heart. "I love The West Wing."

His eyes narrowed. "Who's your favorite character then?"

"Donna." She took a drink. "I love her character arc. How she falls in love with her boss and sticks around despite him neglecting to see her true worth because she's constantly hoping he'll see *her*. But then she discovers her own worth and..."

She sent her hand into the air like a plane taking flight. "Beautiful. And I like CJ. Obvs. What about you?"

"Toby."

"Interesting." She smiled. "Intelligent, quiet, grumpy, and a secretly soft underbelly, eh? How did you get into it? It's quite a dated favorite, pretty old and not something you would have watched as a kid."

"My parents are *huge* fans. They re-watch it every single year. When we were old enough to watch, it became an annual family thing. Molly loves it too. Though she has a crush on Ainsely Hayes. What about you? How did *you* find the West Wing?"

A lump formed in her throat. "My gramps. He's to blame for my entire pop-cultural upbringing."

As though he sensed her sadness, he cleared his throat. "What's next?"

She smiled at the President Bartlet reference. "Star Wars or Star Trek?" She held her breath.

There had to be something wrong with him. He'd bought her books in a bookstore, he was delicious, smelled good enough to eat, complimented her on her karaoke, and he'd kissed her like he owned her. Not liking sci-fi was where the line was, it had to be.

"Wars."

Her stomach fluttered. "Trek. But I'm not averse to Star Wars. I'll watch it. Left handed or right?" He was right handed, the internet had told her so, but it was a fun question to ask all the same.

"Only left handed people ask that question." He pointed his drink at her like it was an accusation.

"Guilty."

"I'm right handed. You didn't answer the first question, what's your favorite TV show?"

"Shadowhunters."

"Never seen it."

She gasped dramatically, smacking the back of her hand against her forehead. "You haven't?" She held up her wrist, showing him the small rune tattoo just under the ball of her thumb.

"What does it mean?"

"Fearless."

His eyes darted between hers. "I can tell."

Something flickered in her chest. "Favorite song?"

"I always envy people who can just pick a song or a book and declare it their favorite."

"What about a genre?"

He shook his head. "I like just about everything except gangster rap."

"I love the oldies."

He pursed his lips. "How old?"

"70's, 80's, 90's."

"Suitably old. Great decades."

"Another round?"

"Please." Will answered for both of them and Jen's waggling eyebrows had another snort bursting from her before she could smother it with her hand. Smooth. Real smooth. Sure, he'd kissed her once, but there was still plenty of time for her to chase him off by, well, being herself.

"Crunchy or smooth peanut butter?" She jabbed a finger at him.

"Smooth."

"Orange juice – smooth or with bits?"

"Uhhh... freshly squeezed and not store bought?"

She scrunched up her face. "You're telling me oranges don't come in cartons from the store? Lies."

His chuckle was golden and made her want to jump up and down with glee. The tension in his muscles was easing, the sadness on his face, too.

She folded her arms. It was make or break time. "And where do we fall on the whole pineapple on pizza debate?" She arched her eyebrow and steeled herself to do battle.

"I don't get why everyone has a problem with pineapple on pizza. I mean. I don't love it. It's not my favorite thing. I don't worship at the temple of pineapple or anything. But I won't crucify you for it either."

She heaved out a breath. "Right answer. Wait – there's a temple of pineapple?"

Another chuckle, longer and more relaxed than the first. Melodic and smooth. "What were the stakes? I feel like I'm on trial."

She grinned. "I don't know that I can be friends with someone who likes crunchy peanut butter, and hates pineapple on pizza. I'd have had to wash my hands of you." She brushed her palms together.

His nostrils flared. "Is that so?"

She nodded.

He leaned closer to her, gliding the pad of his thumb along her jaw. "You'd be done with me even though our kisses taste like that?"

She tilted her head. "Taste like what? I've already forgotten how it tasted. You'll have to remind me."

"Liar."

Her cheeks were hot and her pulse fluttered faster and faster the more he stared at her.

"But I can definitely remind you." He pulled her to him by her waist, an urgency holding her in his grip and a fire burning low in her belly.

Mid-kiss, she pulled back. "How do you take your steak?"

He burst out laughing. "Right now? That's what you need to know right in this moment?"

She shrugged and slipped her hands around his neck. "If you like your steak cooked until it's a hockey puck, or still mooing, we're going to have issues and I need to stop this train."

"I don't. Now, if it's all the same to you, I'm not quite finished kissing you yet."

Her stomach dropped to her feet, her heart took flight, and her fingers burrowed into the soft hair at the nape of his neck.

She wasn't finished kissing him either.

CHAPTER 2

Will

"Early bird or night owl?" She narrowed her eyes again, like whatever was fast-growing between them might be dependent on his every answer.

"Morning."

That earned a nod. She seemed to concur. A pang struck somewhere deep in his chest. Finn was an early bird, too. He missed their morning runs. He missed him, period.

Quinn. He needed to focus on Quinn. It was all less hurty when he stared at her.

She was the most beautiful woman he'd ever seen, and when she looked at him, her green eyes held a concern and a deep sympathy he wished they didn't. She'd clearly read his body language and knew he wasn't at his best, but she at least had the courtesy to keep quiet about it.

She wore an Audrey Hepburn style black dress that flared at her waist and was covered in green polka dots that matched her eyes. She held herself with a confidence that said she didn't give a fuck what the world thought of her, but an endearing thread of vulnerability and uncertainty glimmered within her every now and then as they spoke.

"Tea or coffee?" Her left eye twitched.

"Coffee."

Another nod.

He reached out to stroke her hand that lay next to her on the bar. He couldn't stop himself. Her pale skin was soft, she smelled of honey and cinnamon, and she tasted of impulses and new beginnings.

Being close to her made the aching hurt less. He didn't hate himself as much when she looked at him like he was a decent guy.

"What are you studying?"

She stroked his thumb sending ripples of unfamiliar warmth through his arm. "Gender, women, and sexuality studies."

Huh. That sounded interesting. A world away from his computer science, but diversity was the spice of life. "Favorite sport?" He waited for her response.

She held both hands up in front of her chest. "Don't kill me. It's Formula One racing. My cousin races for one of the teams. He's been racing since he was little and the whole family got sucked in. My dad's a huge fan, and since he never got any boys, I was always his little grease monkey."

His heart swelled at her story.

"Hockey's a close second though. Honest."

"I've never watched a race."

"I'll forgive you." She jabbed a finger at his nose, booping it. "But just this once. Any other questions you get wrong and..." She jerked her thumb across the front of her neck. "Womp, womp. I'll educate you on F1, though. Maybe we can watch a race together some time."

She had to be the most popular girl in school. Smartest, funniest, most beautiful. "Were you prom queen?"

There had never been any chance of him winning prom king in high school; despite playing hockey, he hadn't filled out. His geeky nature made him the butt of people's jokes rather than high on their list of people to vote for. Finn had almost taken the crown, and his friendship had kept Will from taking a beating more than once.

But Quinn... surely she'd blazed a trail through high school, leaving her mark on everyone whose path she crossed.

She snorted and tucked her hair behind her left ear, a fierce blush blooming on her cheeks. "Why would you even ask that?"

"I'm pretty sure you're the most beautiful woman I've ever seen, Quinn. And I've never met someone so easy to talk to."

Her blush darkened. He didn't care that he was full on, he didn't care that he might sound pathetic. Tonight, he could be whoever he wanted to be, and tonight, he wanted to be someone stronger, more confident, someone worthy of a woman like Quinn.

She nibbled on the inside of her lip. "I didn't go to prom. My dad got sick and it just wasn't to be." She shrugged. "I wasn't nearly popular enough to be prom queen, though. I didn't like the right music or TV shows, and my quirky, retro, thrift store clothes weren't the height of fashion." She flicked her hair over her shoulder and wiggled her head back and forth with an eye roll.

She picked up her drink and took a sip, a faraway look settling over her face. "I march to the beat of my own drummer, there's no way I would have been picked. Hell, even my own mother can't stand me."

There was clearly baggage there, but he didn't want to pry. He tipped her chin so her warm, spring green eyes met his. "Well, you'd have been my choice."

She beamed. "You're a charmer, William Morrison. But I'm here for it." She traced the edge of his collar with hesitant fingers before tugging him ever so gently toward her and brushing her lips against his.

His better judgment said to slow down, but he was sick of being sensible, sick of being the reliable, predictable Will who did all the right things and never put a foot out of place. He'd gotten straight A's his entire life, he'd excelled at school and sports, and there he was, propping up a bar, a college graduate with no fucking idea what to do next.

Maybe he needed unpredictable, spur of the moment, impulsive. It seemed to work for his sister. And if Molly could screw around without consequence, why couldn't he?

Another pang in his chest. He missed her, too.

Pushing down his feelings about his sister and best friend, he once again focused every ounce of his attention on Quinn. She was stunning. She was funny, charismatic, and seemed every bit as interested in him as he was her.

Sliding his hand around the curve of her neck, her head lolled to the side and he captured her mouth again. Her desperation met his tongue thrust for thrust as he opened his knees and she stepped closer to his stool.

A demanding, frenetic energy sizzled through his body, crackling the air around them. He couldn't stop – he couldn't pull himself away from her. He needed to be inside her, he needed to make her come apart on his cock with his name falling from her lips.

"William..." Her pouty lips were smudged and her eyes wide as she skimmed her palm down the front of his shirt and tugged on his belt buckle.

He shifted to the edge of the stool and slipped off, standing. Her eyes and actions said "fuck me, now," but he'd gotten just about every single thing wrong lately, and while he was okay doing something out of the ordinary for a change, he had to be sure she was okay with it.

He kissed her again before nibbling his way along her jaw. "Come home with me."

She was nodding before he'd finished speaking. He grabbed his jacket from the back of the stool while she picked up her coat from behind the bar. The bartender closed out both tabs and they signed their receipts in anticipatory silence.

When they'd finished, she slid her palm into his and led him through the bar and out the side door. She walked three feet before stopping, turning to face him, her eyes ablaze, and pushing him back until he hit cold concrete.

She feasted on his mouth like he belonged to her, licking, sucking and biting at his lips like she'd been kissing him forever and she already knew every inch of his body. When she cupped his stiff dick and pressed the heel of her hand against it, he moaned. Gripping her, he turned so her back was against the wall and as his fingers grazed the swell of her breast. She grabbed his hand and shoved it under her dress.

"Are you sure?"

She nodded, a coy smile tugging at her lips as she inched her feet further apart. His head and cock were locked in a fierce battle of resolve. The gentleman he'd been his entire life demanded he slow down and show her the time she deserved. But his dick argued she wanted it every bit as much as he did.

The war raged for only a second as she guided his hand under the damp scrap of fabric at the apex of her thighs. "Please, William."

He speared two fingers inside her, curling them toward her front wall and pressing as she sank onto his hand with a shudder. His thumb found her clit and circled, not worried about teasing, or taking his time, he had one goal, to make the woman come undone.

The closer she got to her orgasm, the louder her little pants and gasps grew, and the faster her hips bucked and jerked against his hand. Her nails dug into his biceps and her head leaned backward as he finger fucked her and kissed her neck.

Her body stopped dead when her climax crashed into her, muscles tense from head to toe, a scream breaking free from her open mouth. When she'd barely finished coming, she turned to face the wall. "Get inside me."

His dick pulsed in his pants. He had a condom in his wallet he changed out every few months but to fuck her right there in the alley next to the bar? Surely she deserved better.

She rocked her hips back, grinding her ass against his crotch. Fuck it.

A minute later, he was sheathed and sliding into her heat. Gritting his teeth, he let out a hiss. It had been a long time since he'd been with a woman and he'd be damned if he was going to embarrass himself by coming on entry.

Sliding his hand around her body, he pulled her hips back far enough from the wall that he could access her clit. Building a rhythm between his dick and his fingers, he grunted with each thrust, praying for her release before her walls squeezing around him had him blowing his load.

He kissed along the back of her shoulder and up the side of her neck as his balls tightened. She twisted to meet his mouth with hers, and he swallowed her moans.

"I'm going to come." His voice was gravely, and he was barely being held together by invisible threads of self-restraint.

She kissed him harder and squeezed her muscles around him as he rutted into her against the side of the building. Somehow, his fingers kept moving and she followed him over the cliff soon after.

When he'd slid out and was tying off the condom her shiny, want-filled eyes met his in the dim light of the alley. "Take me home and do it again."

S unlight peeked through a gap in the curtains of his apartment, dragging him from the depths of a comfortable sleep. Unfamiliar warmth pressed against the side of his body, and a mass of wild red hair lay splayed across his chest.

He cringed. While Quinn was a beautiful woman and an interesting person to talk to, one night stands weren't his jam, and until he figured out what the hell he wanted from life, he wasn't in a position to offer her anything more than what they'd already done.

She sighed, hot air blowing onto his arm and sending a shiver through him. That was, assuming she wanted anything more from him, anyway.

Flings were all well and good on the night, but the next day it almost always consisted of awkwardly fishing your pants off a stranger's floor like a hooker.

Except she wasn't a stranger. And she certainly wasn't a hooker. If anything, it was technically a second date. He'd met her before, at the bookstore; he'd bought her books and they'd chatted. As her body rose and fell with even breaths, his muscles softened. He didn't regret taking her to bed, but there were definitely negative feelings swirling in his chest.

"I can hear you overthinking things from here." Her sleepy, mumbled voice was punctuated by a low groan. "Your loud brain woke me up."

He smiled, but didn't quite know how to respond. He'd never been with anyone who had been able to call him out for his overthinking mind before – everyone just assumed he was quiet.

She shifted her weight, and a warm hand wrapped around his morning wood with a satisfied hum. She pumped his length with clear intent, as he fought hard to combat the welling emotions inside him.

His muscles tightened, and a bitter taste rose in the back of his throat. He closed his eyes and tried to breathe through the panic rising in his chest.

But he couldn't shake it.

Clamping his hand over the top of hers, he slowed her to a stop, ignoring her whimpering pleas to let her finish.

Instead, he pushed aside the discomfort and slid down the bed, rolling her flat onto her back, hooking her legs over his shoulders and feasting on her like a man starved.

An hour later, he made coffee while Quinn flipped French toast on a skillet. "You wanna talk about those loud thoughts of yours?"

He sighed and raked a hand through his messy hair. Maybe talking to a stranger would make him feel better about his discomfort.

"I'm embarrassed to say I have no fucking clue what to do now that I've left college." He gestured at a pile of letters on the chair next to her. "I have offers for post-grads, jobs across the country... good jobs, great jobs, jobs other people in my position would kill for, but I just... I don't know what to choose."

He poured the coffee into two mugs and placed them on the table, before turning back to grab the creamer and sugar. "Even this apartment is temporary. My lease is short-term until I figure out what the hell I'm going to do. I feel like I should just... *know*, y'know?"

He dropped onto a chair with a dramatic thud on the table, and she handed him a plate stacked high with thick slices of French toast, cream, and maple syrup.

"It sounds to me like you don't know what you *should* do."

He raised his eyebrow. He'd literally just said that.

"So tell me." She slid onto the chair facing him. "What do you *want* to do?"

His heart stuttered. While Mom and Dad were the most supportive and loving parents he could ever ask for, he'd always felt a pressure to succeed, to make them proud, to help provide for them when they got older.

Was it really as simple as doing something *he* wanted to do? Something he loved?

He opened his mouth to answer, but found there were no words to say. Other than hockey with his brothers, did he even know what brought him joy?

CHAPTER 3
Quinn

Quinn hadn't asked a complicated question, but his dumbfounded face, and the silence consuming the space between them suggested he'd never really considered doing something he loved after college.

He blinked, twice, three times, fork paused mid-air on the way to his mouth, but no sound came from his parted lips.

"It's okay if you don't know." She gave a nervous laugh. "You don't have to have it all figured out. You're barely even out of college. For some people it just takes them a while to find their calling. It's no big deal." She sliced off a forkful of French toast and slipped it into her mouth.

"What do *you* want to do when you graduate?"

She smiled at him and gave a half-shrug. "It depends on the day to be honest. I volunteer for a women's shelter and do a lot of fundraising for them. It's something I love doing. I've considered going into counseling, too."

He sipped his coffee and frowned. "But it's not what sets your heart on fire."

She cocked her head at his perception. "I'd love to own a

bakery." Studying his face, she didn't miss the twitching muscle in his cheek as he clasped the mug in his hands. "I'd love to make cupcakes and treats all day, serve good coffee to people who need a spark of joy in their daily lives."

Pausing for a beat, she speared another chunk of bread on her fork. "I'd love to have a book area too, with oversized seats and a safe space for people to read whatever is in their heart to read. A smut friendly book café and bakery." There, she'd said it out loud.

His face was unreadable, so she dropped her gaze to her plate and waved her fork. "It's just a silly dream. It would be a waste of my studies."

"And it probably wouldn't really help anyone. So why wouldn't you use the degree you've spent so much time and money earning to do something meaningful?"

Her stomach dropped, hardening as it hit the tiled floor like a brick. "People find meaning in all kinds of places." Her voice was flat. Who the hell was he to judge her dreams? He barely even knew her and there he was, passing judgment on something she'd wanted to do since she'd visited her first cupcakery at five years old.

The place had seemed magical to a little girl – all the colors, sprinkles, and edible glitter. When she'd taken a bite out of her enormous cupcake, her tongue had exploded with sweet deliciousness. She'd wanted to eat cupcakes every day thereafter, it was the epitome of sheer joy for her littler self.

"It'll probably never even happen. It's just something I'd like to do." Why did she feel a need to defend herself and her innermost desires to him? Flaring her nostrils, she shook her head.

"Well..." His fork scraped across the plate as he dragged a piece of French toast through the pool of maple syrup. "I guess since you're impulsive enough for a hookup with me, you're not really any more able to commit to the big stuff than I am."

Her insides froze and shattered. The asshole was doubling down. He had no fucking clue what he wanted to do, what his own dreams were, and he had the nerve to suggest she couldn't commit to hers?

Wait. Did he just slut shame her, too? The asshole picked her up at the bar and asked her to go home with him, and *she* was the impulsive one?

She frowned, studying him as he continued to tuck into his food as though he didn't just insult her on multiple levels. The French toast in her mouth withered and stuck in her throat like dry cardboard. She placed her silverware on the plate and straightened her spine.

She didn't need to sit there and take shit from some holier-than-thou asshole she barely knew. She wouldn't even take that shit from people she'd known her whole fucking life. So what if he was tall, dark, handsome, and had a tongue that made her soul leave her body? She deserved respect, and if he wasn't going to respect her, she wasn't sticking around.

She forced her voice to remain calm and steady while her insides raged. "I should get going."

Will

Quinn's warmth and amiable nature had dissipated in the blink of an eye, leaving behind a vast frozen tundra expanding between them. Her jaw was firm, her eyes hard, and every muscle in her body seemed tense. What the fuck had happened?

She scraped her chair along the tiles as she stood. "It was good to see you again, Will."

Good? It had been fucking great. He generally wasn't one to brag, but unless she was faking it, he'd given her a number of back-arching, cuss-screaming orgasms. He'd had his fair share of them as well.

His frown deepened a notch as she stood. "I'll walk you out."

"It's fine. I remember the way."

'It's fine' never meant it was fine. He'd learned that from the guys on his team. And something definitely didn't *feel* fine.

As she walked herself out of the apartment, he combed back over their discussion, frantically trying to figure out where he'd gone wrong and what he'd said to upset her. The cool indifference with which her eyes swept over him as she turned to pull the door behind her, raked over his heart.

What the fuck had happened? Was his uncertainty about his future that much of a turnoff that she had to haul ass in the middle of a perfectly nice breakfast?

He'd only been agreeing with her about there being pros and cons on both sides of her arguments – maybe she'd taken that wrong, somehow?

Or maybe someone as put together as Quinn, someone as sure of herself, someone who knew what she wanted from life, even if she wasn't confident she would bring it to fruition, had no time for someone like him. Hell, she even had a backup plan of counseling, or a paid position at the shelter to fall back on, which was something else she enjoyed doing.

She'd lit up when she'd talked about both baking and the shelter: no matter which she pursued he had no doubt that she'd not only knock it out of the park, but she'd end up happy.

Maybe he should have told her that he wasn't a complete lowlife living off his parents. He was a self-sustaining adult, who was just a little lost. Sure, he felt more than a little lost, but perhaps he should have comforted her with the fact he did plan to do *something*.

He had his own place, his own car, his own money. He'd designed and sold games and apps over the years that had left him with a tidy sum in the bank, enough to get him through a few months of uncertainty.

But at the end of the day, the money from his side-hustle would run out if he didn't figure out what he wanted to do for his main-hustle, and take the right steps to make it happen.

She'd seemed so encouraging at first, telling him it was okay to not have a clue what he wanted to do. But if she was so quietly judgmental about the fact he couldn't settle on any of his prospects, maybe it was for the best that they parted ways after what was arguably the best night of his freakin' life.

Quinn

Quinn didn't even take a Lyft back to her apartment. She stomped through the streets, righteous indignation dripping from every step she took. What. An. Asshole.

She slammed the door behind her. Sweat coursed down her face and neck, and pooled in the small of her back.

Her roomie and best friend, Sabrina, looked up from her bowl of cereal. "Did you go running in that?" She pointed her spoon at Quinn's dress.

Quinn didn't answer, instead, she made her way into the kitchen, opened the liquor cabinet and poured herself a shot of the first glass bottle her hand fell on.

"What in the world?"

Quinn downed the shot and poured another before pulling a second glass and pouring Sabrina a drink.

"Friends don't let friends do morning shots alone." In truth, Bre was more like family. In the absence of Quinn having any real relationship with her blood-born-family, Bre was the family she'd chosen.

Sabrina picked up her shot. "Friends might, but ride-or-die besties wouldn't." She raised her glass. "First we drink, then you talk. Then you pick up some of those piles of books lying around this place. I almost broke my toe on your latest purchases."

Quinn flattened her lips and nodded. "You drive a hard bargain, Bre. But, deal."

"Correction." Sabrina screwed up her face. "First we drink, then you shower, *then* you talk."

"Would you believe me if I told you I already had a shower this morning?"

"A sweat shower?"

Quinn laughed, some of the knots easing in her shoulders. "Fuck the patriarchy." She tipped her shot back into her mouth and swallowed down the fiery lemon vodka.

Bre followed suit and slammed her glass onto the counter, bending at the waist. "It burns." When she stood, her eyes watered. "There's a reason people work up to doing shots on a night out, Quinny."

Quinn placed the bottle back in the cupboard and dropped both shot glasses into the sink before pulling open the fridge and grabbing the orange juice. She chugged it for a few seconds before wiping her mouth with the back of her hand.

"There, now it's a vodka mimosa. Happy?"

Sabrina shook her head. "What gives? Who activated your sassy button this morning?"

Quinn picked up last night's leftovers from the fridge and speared the sundried tomato pasta salad with a fork like it had done her wrong.

"Isn't my sassy always activated?" She flicked her hair. "Comes with the territory of being a temperamental redhead, remember?"

"Not like this." Bre sat back down and scooped another mouthful of cereal. "Someone did this."

After a few moments stabbing spirals of pasta and cramming them into her mouth, Quinn's jaw ached from the aggressive chewing. "I went home with someone last night."

"You don't say..." Sabrina picked up her bowl and drank the excess milk, wiping a drop from her chin. "Don't you always storm around town dressed to the nines on a Wednesday morning? Aren't you in heels? Didn't that hurt like hell?"

"It fueled my hate fire."

Bre didn't miss a beat, or the movie reference. "We should watch that this weekend. Maybe a dose of Pitch Perfect 2 will help you calm the hell down from whatever guy has you this twisted up."

"Will Morrison." She dropped her head to the table and groaned, waiting for Sabrina's reaction. Three... two...

"You didn't."

"Oh. I did. Repeatedly."

Bre's comedic gasp was worth it. "Repeatedly? Are you dating him?"

"No ma'am. I just fucked him. A lot."

"I didn't know you were seeing him last night." Sabrina's jaw still hung open and her eyes were wide.

"Neither did I. He was at Pucks."

Sabrina's eyes grew wider. "For karaoke? Alone?" Her voice rose in pitch with each question.

"To be honest I'm not sure he knew what day it was. He was pretty down."

"So you cheered him up with your vagina?" Sabrina took a sip of tea before scrunching up her nose. "Cold." She got up, and hit the button on the kettle, turned to face Quinn and opened her arms as if to say, 'well? Are you going to get to it?'

"Two women were eyeing him like he was a piece of meat at a Fourth of July barbecue. So I stepped in to protect him since he just seemed so... sad." She shrugged.

"And *then* you cheered him up with your vagina?"

"I'll have you know that *he* kissed *me* first."

Sabrina rubbed her eyes with the heels of her hand. "What the hell bizarro universe is this?"

"Quality Buffy reference." She held out her closed fist for Bre to bump.

"Will made a move on you last night? Will... Morrison? Mr. Socially Awkward, and to my knowledge never dates?"

Quinn replaced the lid on the tub. "Will Morrison made a number of moves on me last night, and then again this morning."

Bre strode to the door of the kitchen and peered around it. "Where are the camera crews? You have to be shitting me right now." On her walk back to the table, she paused, made another cup of tea before sitting back on her seat.

"No shitting. We weren't drunk, either. I mean we had a few drinks, but we didn't get trashed or anything. No shots."

"I mean, if anyone was going to bring out Will's assertiveness it would be you. Russell said the guys had never seen him walk straight up to a woman and talk to you the way he did at the bookstore. But... wow."

"He kissed me in the bar, asked me to go home with him."

If Bre's eyebrows rose any higher, they were going to shoot into the atmosphere.

Quinn's face heated as she continued in a whisper. "He fucked me against the wall of the bar in the alley."

"He didn't! Now I know you're making shit up."

Quinn nodded, her body flaring at the memory. "He did. And it was so fucking hot, Bre. So fucking hot. Possibly the best lay I've ever had. But when we woke up this morning he wouldn't even let me give him a hand job. He slipped under the covers and..." She waved her hand in the direction of her crotch like she didn't need to elaborate.

"This is... I can't... So... wait... What went wrong?" Bre blurted out her question on an exaggerated sigh.

"He slut shamed me. Told me that since I was impulsive enough to have a one night stand, that it stood to reason that I couldn't decide on whether I wanted to go into counseling or open a bakery."

The shift in Bre's face from sheer wide-mouth shock to fury was instant. "He fucking did not. Who does that?"

Quinn nodded. "Oh, he fucking did." Her heart sank. Under the thick layer of burning anger, his words had cut her to the bone. She'd liked him, both at the bookstore and at the bar, and while she wasn't looking for wedding bells and picket fences any time soon, she had wanted to see him again.

She'd thought their one night stand might have been the start of something more, something deeper, something special. Ugh. She groaned at her own naivety.

"I'm sorry." Bre reached over and picked up her hand, cradling it between her palms. "I know you liked him." She flicked her gaze to the floor.

"What is it?"

Sabrina shook her head. "I didn't think you'd pursue anything with him, so I didn't think I should mention it. But now... I... You know I don't like to gossip." Her voice was barely a whisper.

"But?"

"But this isn't the first time he's slut shamed someone. Molly—"

"His own sister?" Quinn's blood was reaching boiling point. "You're kidding me?"

Sabrina shook her head, squeezing Quinn's hand before pulling back. "I wish I was, Quinny. I'm not sure how he's so antifeminist when his parents are so strongly supportive of Molly. But something's not quite right there. He just... He's so judgmental of what she wears and does with her body."

"Russ says that every rookie on the team got warned to stay the hell away from her." She sipped her tea. "It was why she and Finn took so damn long to get together. And speaking of them being together, Will lost his *shit* when he found out."

"Was that at the grad party last weekend?"

Bre nodded. "Yeah. Russ said they're still not okay. Finn is furious about how Will treated Molly, and Will is hurt and betrayed that they kept it a secret from him."

"No excuse to be a mondo cock about the whole thing."

"Accurate statement. I don't know what his deal is, but he seems to have a thing about controlling women. Or at least Molly. I don't know what he's like in a relationship."

A one-off comment to her that could have been explained away by awkwardness, or not realizing what he said was one thing, but knowing about his behavior toward his own sister, made it a pattern. One Quinn wasn't about to fall into. She lifted her cup to Bre. "And I'm sure as hell not going to find out."

CHAPTER 4

Will

"He's what?"

"Leaving." Linc repeated himself as he tipped sugar into the huge mug in front of him.

"Johnny White?" Will had been coerced into having coffee with his boys. Minus Finn. A twinge spiked his heart. His tribe – minus his ride or die – had shown up at his door and waited for him to get dressed and go out with them. "For real this time? He's been threatening it for a while."

They had promised they'd physically manhandle him out of his apartment if he didn't go to the *Sugar Bean* willingly. So there he was, sipping his cappuccino. "I can't believe he's finally doing it. Where's he going?"

"'Bama." Russ's answer was laced with amusement.

"What am I missing? Why is that funny?" He shoved half a croissant in his mouth and chewed.

Austin drained his glass of water. "I believe the humor lies in the fact that Johnny is transferring to a team where one of his teammates is dating his ex-girlfriend. But I could be mistaken."

Russ laughed harder. "I hope that asshole gets what he

deserves. He's someone else's problem now. Glory hunting motherfucker waiting to win a championship before making the switch. Way to abandon the team."

"Speaking of team... We should have a party for him leaving." Linc was always the diplomatic one in the group.

Russ clutched his ribs. "Good luck or good riddance?"

"Yes." Lincoln nodded, his lips twitching. "He's been a good player on the ice."

"And a raging asshole off of it." Russ sniffed and shook his head. "Good riddance, for sure."

As outgoing team captain it should have been him planning any leaving festivities. "I'll do it."

"You sure?" Linc quirked a brow.

"I'm sure. It's not like I'm doing anything else these days." Ouch. Pity party for one. A beat of awkward silence fell heavily over the table.

Russ produced a notebook from the bench next to him and slapped it onto the table with a dramatic thud. Linc dropped a pen on top. "We can all help out."

Will snorted. Most college students would have ordered a keg and cake and called it good, but not the Snow Pirates. No. Even for a bullying asshole like Johnny White they didn't half ass things. It was something he'd always been proud of, no matter what they faced, they did it with their whole entire asses.

His heart twitched. Finn was the life and soul of the party, and while they'd declared peace and were attempting to move forward with their brolationship, things were still just... off.

He'd tried messaging them but they weren't replying. When they did, it was just one word responses. He'd tried to arrange to hang out, but Finn had turned him down.

He had no one to blame but himself. *He* was the one who'd managed to drive them away by being an absolute asshole. He cringed at the memory. How his team had held themselves back and not given him a beating in the middle of his parents' kitchen was anyone's guess. He'd deserved it, then and still.

He couldn't blame Finn and Molly if they never forgave him. He deserved that, too.

Laughter to his left pulled him out of beating himself over the recent past. What he wouldn't give for some good times and laughter with his sister and his best friend.

Quinn sat at a table with Sabrina – who had given Russ a pretty intense kiss when he'd arrived at the coffee shop, drawing hoots and whistles from their group. Quinn's head was thrown back, hysterical laughter shaking her entire body. Will couldn't help but stare.

A notepad lay between the two women on the table, and a pack of multicolored pens were open and scattered in between coffee cups and side plates with half eaten desserts on them.

"Will?"

He turned his head slowly back toward Linc, not wanting to tear his eyes away from her. "Yeah?"

"Ask the woman out."

He couldn't. He'd flown too close to the sun and she'd singed him. He couldn't afford to go down in a blaze, even if that blaze was Quinn Richards. Though the more he saw her, the more enticing it sounded.

"I think they're planning Quinn's next fundraiser." Russ picked up his coffee and took a drink. "If you wanted to, you could go over there and offer some ideas." He gave a casual shrug but his eyes pinned Will with a look that said he knew.

Girls talked. Quinn had undoubtedly talked to Sabrina about their night together the previous week. Had Sabrina then told Russ? Probably. Maybe he'd know why Quinn went from warm and fuzzy to subzero in a split second. Will quirked an eyebrow. Would he tell? Would he send Will into the lion's den to watch Quinn tear him limb from limb for his own amusement?

Linc chuckled. "She doesn't bite."

"She may." Austin smirked. "But he may also enjoy it."

He'd skated on the ice in games against men twice his size who hated him with way more passion than Quinn. Surely he could handle going over to say hi. His legs were already moving. He crossed the space and stood awkwardly next to their table, tucking his hands in his jean pockets.

"Hey."

Quinn slowly pulled her gaze from Sabrina, and cool green eyes met his. "Will."

Something twisted in his gut. He liked her calling him William. But from the firm set of her lips and the flaring of her nostrils, *William* was the last person she wanted to see.

"Hey Will." Sabrina gave a small wave and a sympathetic smile. "I'm going for a refill. You want anything, Quinny?"

Without taking her eyes off his face she answered. "I could go for another shot of caffeine."

"Will?"

"Thanks, but I'm good."

When Sabrina moved toward the counter, he gestured at the chair. "Can I sit for a second?"

She continued to glare at him, but didn't object when he took a seat. "I'm sorry. I was a jerk. I upset you and I didn't mean to."

He still wasn't sure what he was apologizing for, but as long as she didn't prod him for clarification on what, specifically, he was sorry about, he could ask her at another time when the eyes of his teammates weren't piercing his back.

Her eyes narrowed, and he knew he was fucked. She leaned back, folded her arms, and asked what he was sorry for.

Scraping his hands through his hair he shook his head.

"I'm honestly not sure." His stomach coiled. She was going to punch him. And worse? He was sure he deserved it.

"You shamed me for hooking up with you and dismissed my dreams." Her voice was layered with venom and while her words were English and a complete sentence, he couldn't remember having said anything of the sort.

Was he really that much of an asshole? He opened his mouth, but didn't know what to say. He scrubbed the back of his neck with a clammy palm and searched her pale face. Her hard eyes had turned sad and she chewed the inside of her cheek.

Things were definitely getting out of hand. The things that were in his brain versus what was coming from his mouth weren't matching up and were hurting people. *He* was hurting people. First Molly, now Quinn.

"You told me I should do something worthwhile with my degree, like opening a bakery wasn't worthwhile."

Shit. He had said that. "That's not exactly what I meant."

"Maybe not, but it's what you said. And I don't know you well enough to know what you mean and don't mean. I don't live in your brain, Will."

She had a point.

"Can we agree that next time I open my big mouth and say something offensive you'll smack me upside the head and tell me to knock it off? Because I'm pretty sure it'll happen again no matter how hard I try to avoid it." He shook his head. "I swear I'm not a dick on purpose."

"I wasn't trying to put you down. And I certainly wasn't trying to make you feel bad for hooking up with me." He turned to make sure his friends weren't eavesdropping and they all jumped and turned away like something from a movie, quickly becoming invested in whatever was on Linc's phone screen.

"I guess I was projecting. My uncertain future..." His

stomach swirled. He wanted to share with her that he felt dirty about a one night stand, but he didn't want to get into the why, especially not where his friends might hear.

She must have seen his dismay but he wasn't letting up, not that he blamed her. "You hurt me."

"I'm sorry."

They held each other's gaze for a moment before anyone spoke. Sabrina returned to the table with coffees and a long, girl-stare he couldn't decipher passed between the two women.

He shifted awkwardly in his seat. "Russ says you're coming up with fundraising ideas. For the women's center, right?"

She nodded, and her eyes lit up. "We do a few throughout the year. This one's a biggie. I'm doing a bake sale, obviously." Her cheeks flushed and his stomach dropped at having ever made her feel bad about something that set her soul on fire. "But I wanted something else to run alongside it."

"She's an overachiever." Sabrina blew the foam across the top of her mug before taking a tentative sip. "The charity coordinator left and Quinn has stepped in to help out until they can officially fill the position. She wants to make a splash and set the bar impossibly high for the person who fills the role."

Quinn's eyes flashed. "If I were to work at the shelter after graduation, it would be the role I'd want. I love to plan parties and raise money for a good cause." She rubbed her chest. "And what can I say? I have a competitive streak a mile long."

That was something he understood. "How about an auction?"

"We did one of those last year. And I saw another local charity just held a huge auction. It might be hard to get things to auction from local businesses right now. But I could try."

Will turned back to his teammates who were watching the exchange and probably trying to overhear every word. Served them right that he was about to throw them all under a bus. "How about auctioning off dates with the local college hockey team?"

They were going to kill him. But at least if he was dead, it would mean he wouldn't have to go out on a date with someone he didn't know – even if it was for charity, even if it was for *Quinn's* charity.

Her eyes lit up again and she jerked to look at Sabrina whose eyes were wide. Sabrina shrugged like she didn't care that they wanted to auction off her boyfriend, but glanced at the guys behind him. "They're going to kill you."

"Cleo might kill him." Quinn tapped her pen on her chin.

He hadn't thought it through. They all might kill him. "Uh... It's for a good cause." Heat crept up his neck and into his cheeks. "What's a little death between friends when it comes to something so important?"

They were going to know he had it bad for Quinn, but at this point he didn't care. He'd hurt her and he wanted to fix it – he *needed* to fix it. He wanted to spend more time with her, getting to know her, letting her get to know him. He wanted to see her eyes sparkle and her face light up with joy.

Ugh. He was such a goner for the woman. The guys were never letting him live it down.

"I'm sure they won't mind too much. They get to help out a local charity and look good doing it. Those asshats love any excuse to dress up." He doubled down on throwing them under a bus with such ease, he surprised even himself. They'd seem like even worse assholes than he was if they said no to the event now.

"And you?" Quinn flicked her pen back and forward, thwapping it off the notepad on the table as she pinned him with a questioning stare.

"What about me?"

"You'll be in the auction too?"

"Of course. As outgoing captain, I'll consider it my last duty to the Snow Pirates." He smiled at her, though his insides withered at the idea of being on display in a room full of people. "I can't let my boys have all the fun."

She tapped her lip with the end of the pen, and he slipped his hands under his ass to save from reaching out and touching them. Or worse, embarrassing himself by trying to kiss her in front of all of their friends.

He was under no illusions, she hadn't forgiven him simply because he'd said sorry. Hurt didn't work like that. Especially when he doled out such craptastic apologies. Saying one word didn't magically erase the harm done from what he'd said. He couldn't put the toothpaste back in the tube.

He'd learned from everything with Molly and Finn that a simple 'I'm sorry' wasn't the magic pill to fix everything. No matter how badly he wished it was. Time and hard work would hopefully rectify things with his sister and best friend, and with Quinn...

Her glinting eyes assessed him and softened. Maybe he hadn't irreparably fucked up. Maybe there was some part of her that wanted a do over as much as he did.

CHAPTER 5

Quinn

"**N**o." Quinn tossed a throw pillow at Bre, who sat on her bed with a textbook on her lap and a highlighter crammed between her teeth.

"You've said that already."

"And I meant it every single time I said it before. I'm not going to Johnny White's leaving party. The guy's an asshole and I'm glad to see him go." She also didn't want to see Will, but she didn't want to say it out loud, not even to her bestie.

"You and everyone else in school. I think it's the only reason people are showing up, because they want to make sure he's actually leaving and this isn't some kind of cruel joke." Sabrina jabbed her highlighter at Quinn. "But that's not the real reason you don't want to go."

Ugh. She hated how well Bre knew her.

"It's not?" No matter how much she tried to force calm into her voice, it came out strained. So they both knew she was avoiding Will. Bre wouldn't leave it at that. She sucked in a deep breath, readying herself for the inevitable best friend lecture.

"You can lie to yourself all you want, but I'm not buying that BS. You're avoiding Will."

There was no use denying it. "Fine. Yes. But I have to." She folded her arms, hoping the action would strengthen her resolve not to go and ogle his delicious cognac eyes and easy smile. Every time she pictured his face, she wanted to slide her fingers through his hair and nibble on his jaw and earlobe.

Sabrina threw the pillow back and it landed on her chest, a huff of air escaping her on impact. "You're thinking about him now. I can tell from the dreamy look on your face and that blush blooming on your cheeks." She wagged the neon green pen. "You like him."

"This is why I have to avoid him. I can't think straight when he's in my space. My vagina gets all kinds of ideas about him, and I am powerless to fight against his magnetism."

"His magnetism to your vagina?"

Quinn gave a somber nod. "He's a jerk. We don't hold space for slut shamers. We just don't. I know he said sorry, but he's still a serial offender and I'm not okay with his shitty attitude. Sorry doesn't fix all of that, y'know?"

"But?"

Quinn glanced at her crotch, the image of him between her legs burned into her memory forever.

"Vagina magnetism?" Sabrina *got* her.

"Vagina magnetism."

"I still think you should come to the party. There will be other people there and I can run interference. I'm sure Cleo wouldn't mind helping make sure your vagina magnet doesn't lead you into Will's pants again."

But she wanted back in Will's pants. He seemed genuine, sweet and kind. She didn't for a second think he was a deliberate asshole, but she knew enough to know to keep her distance. He'd hurt her too deep, too fast, and she really didn't want to give him the chance to do it again, or somehow hurt her even worse.

And yet...

"From the looks of it, your vagina magnet isn't getting the memo."

"Ugh." She covered her face with her forearms and flopped back onto the bed. "Traitorous wench."

"You have an hour before we need to leave. I suggest you take the edge off with one of your many vibrators. Wear something complicated to get into – no easy access for quickies. Underwear is a requirement not an option. If you're really intent on not seeing him I'd even suggest no make-up – you'll hide from him just fine if you thought he'd see you without make up."

Sabrina paused and made eye contact. "Not that I think he'd care. I think he's gone for you, too, Quinny. I know we have issues with his attitude, I do. But I also think that boy is book boyfriend level invested in you: hearts in his eyes, shy smiles... heck, he even volunteered the whole hockey team to help you raise money for a cause close to your heart."

"You know she can hear you, right?" Quinn pointed at her crotch. She grabbed a throw pillow and smacked it onto her abdomen. A vain attempt that it would somehow prevent her vagina from hearing her best friend say nice things about the penis owner she wanted to sink between her thighs again. "Don't listen to Bre. She doesn't know what she's talking about. Will Morrison is to be avoided at all costs tonight, you hear me?"

Sabrina smirked as though she knew better. Quinn wasn't fooling anyone. But she was going to the party, she was going to do her level best to hide from Will, and if she managed to make it home unscathed it would be a fucking miracle.

Party in full swing at the hockey house, so far so good. She'd managed to stay out of Will's way, watching him from a distance as he hung out with his friends. Someone had bought a sheet cake that said 'Good Luck' at the start of the night, but it now read: 'Good fucking riddance.'

She couldn't help but admire the graffiti artist's determination to deface the cake. Their handwriting with frosting was kind of impressive too, neat, legible, and not to mention Johnny was a bully and the student body would be better off with him gone. So she also couldn't blame them for wanting him to know exactly how they felt about his leaving.

She couldn't help but feel sorry for Alabama though. Johnny had failed his freshman year and retaken it, changed his major and minor more times than anyone could count, and he was seemingly set on being an eternal student.

He kept his grades to the minimum requirement for hockey, and he was good, really good. She suspected it was why he got to fuck around so much in other areas.

She wouldn't wish him on anyone.

"Admiring the handiwork?"

Oh God. Busted. He'd found her. And his voice. His presence near her back. His warmth. His smell. It all made her dizzy.

"I mean, it's not as good as mine – obviously."

"Obviously." He stepped closer, his breath tickling her bare shoulder and his chest grazing her back. She had listened to Sabrina and worn jeans, but she'd also worn an off-the-shoulder shirt that made her tits look great and flattered her hourglass figure.

"But there's a certain somethin' somethin' lacking in the decoration, don't you think?" She flashed him a smile over her shoulder, wishing she hadn't fallen into his trap and met his eyes. His delicious, intense brown eyes that hid nothing and told her everything.

Yeah. She was epically fucked.

"I think whoever did it is an incredibly talented artist." His lips wiggled as though he was fighting a laugh. He knew who'd defaced the cake.

"Did you do this?" She thrusted her finger at the table.

"I deeply regret that I didn't think of it first." He grinned and her underwear melted.

"I said no thanks." A distressed voice made her spin on her heels to find a woman trying to jerk her hand out of a guy's grasp. She didn't recognize the guy, but the woman's face was twisted in fear and panic. Before she could step forward, Will was already moving.

He draped his arm over her shoulder with an ease that radiated warmth. "Hey baby, sorry I'm late." Frowning, he turned his attention to the guy. "Do you even go to school here?"

The stranger glowered and clenched his teeth but stayed silent.

"You should probably leave, don't you think?"

"I'm a friend of Johnny's. This party is for him, isn't it?"

Will didn't back down despite the guy having at least 50lbs on him and standing a few inches taller than him too.

"Well, I'm the captain of the team and you just inappropriately grabbed my girl, so I'm going to have to ask you to leave before I – and some of my teammates – escort you out the door."

The guy tipped his chin. "You threatening me?"

"I'm saying your brand of flirting doesn't belong here at the U. Leave, before we make you."

Why was it so hot watching a guy defend a woman's honor? Women had fought for the right to vote, and they'd spent years attempting to overthrow the myth that women needed men's protection, but when a man squared up to another guy to protect a woman?

Phew. That did things to her. Which, in turn, made her want to do things to him.

The confident, confrontational, protector Will in front of her was a world away from the geeky, awkward quiet man she'd slept with.

He'd jumped to her defense without a second thought, putting himself between the trembling woman and the asshole. Quinn backed away from the situation, scanning the room for Sabrina, or Cleo, or a 'break glass in case of emergency' thingy that she could smash as a means of escape before her panties burst into flames.

Her clit throbbed, and she ached to taste him again. When she closed her eyes to ground herself, the ghost of his fingertips drifted across her skin, sending ripples of need to her core. She needed to get out. She needed to go home, pour herself a gin and Sprite, grab a block of cheese and a box of crackers, curl up in her Snuggie and binge watch the shit out of something until Netflix asked if she was still watching.

Instead, she watched as Will and Linc walked the stranger out and locked the door behind him. She watched as he checked that the woman was okay and grabbed ice and a Ziploc for her already bruising arm. And she watched as he glanced around the room, searching for his target like a heat-seeking missile, smiling when he met her gaze and stalked toward her.

Her breath caught as he cupped her face with his palm and his lips met hers with a fierce hunger that almost shredded her heart where she stood. She balled his shirt in her fist, pulling him to her, wanting everything he was willing to give.

"Need... to... leave..." Her words tumbled out between desperate kisses, and he nodded against her forehead.

He led her to get her coat, waited for her to say goodbye to a scowling Sabrina, and kept his hand on her lower back as he guided her through the mass of loud, dancing bodies, testing the capacity of the hockey house.

At his car, he kissed her again, deep, demanding, yet somehow still tender. His hard length pressed against her abdomen as he pinned her to the side of the car. She couldn't wait to get back to either of their beds. She needed him, urgently.

"Now."

"Now." He nodded. "Back seat?"

She was already moving to open the door but stopped and he collided with her back. Spinning to face him, she jabbed his chest with an accusing index finger. "I swear to God, William, if you slut shame me for what we're about to do, I will cut off your dick with a rusty blade, drive to the zoo, and feed it to wild animals."

His eyes widened, and he held up his hands. "No slut shaming. I didn't even mean to the last time."

The tension seeped out of his every muscle, as though he was physically struggling to keep a handle on his lust. She took a moment to revel in his discomfort. It intoxicated her to know that his need to be inside her matched her own.

Picking up his hand with her left, she waggled the index finger of her right. "I mean it. If you make me feel so much as unclean for having sex in the back seat of your car, I will hurt you."

He nodded. "I believe you. And the fact you've given it so much thought to the point you have a game plan for if I fuck up again is not only terrifying, but makes me want to take care of you. I really am sorry I ever made you feel like you were anything but a goddess."

She nibbled on her lip and squinted at him before sliding his hand down her stomach and into the band of her pants.

With his free hand, he popped the button and zipper open, and she widened her stance.

Tipping her head back, she let out a low moan as his fingers found the hot, wet mess between her thighs.

"Fuck. You're soaking."

She nodded, gasping as he rolled her slippery clit between his thumb and forefinger. He drove all rational sense and reason out of her mind. She didn't care that they were parked around the corner from the hockey house. She didn't care that college kids milled about. She didn't care that they stood under a street light. Hell, she didn't even care that she was supposed to be keeping her distance.

Her vagina magnet was turned on and at full power. She was its minion, helpless to fight the tug toward the gorgeous man offering her another mind blowing orgasm. If he'd stripped her naked where she stood, she'd have let him. Instead, she kicked off her shoes and dropped her ass to the edge of the back seat.

Shucking off her pants and underwear and tossing them into the footwell, she opened her legs. Car sex was never as sexy as it looked on TV, trying to get things where they needed to be in such a confined space was tricky – but she didn't care about that, nor the exhibitionism either. She just needed him inside her.

She circled her clit while he unbuttoned his pants, freed his dick, and sheathed it. Pumping his leaking cock as he watched her, he sighed. "You're so beautiful, Quinn."

Flashing him a wicked grin, she walked her toes up the outside of his thighs and pulled. "Get in here and fuck me, William."

He climbed into the car, somehow pulling the door shut behind him and settled between her legs. The confined space served only to drive them closer together. She clung to him as he angled his way inside her, hissing out a breath as he gripped her hips and dragged her toward him to deepen his access.

At first, he didn't move, just stared, cock inside her aching, hot pussy. Peeling her shirt up her chest, he freed her tits from the pastel, floral lace bra and glided his fingers over her perky nipples.

She sighed, clenching her walls around him. While she could lie there all night and let him worship her, she needed a quick fuck to take the edge off so they could get back to his place and enjoy each other all the more.

She tilted her hips and groaned. "Will, please."

Leaning over her body, he nipped at her breast. "William. I like when you call me William."

"Then fuck me and I'll say it. Until then, it's Will." She frowned and he chuckled but drove his hips toward hers, once, twice, painfully slowly, before picking up speed with each thrust. He wasn't particularly big, or girthy, but that didn't stop him from hitting where she needed him to.

Slipping her arms around his neck, she held him against her, playing with his hair as he fucked her.

"Harder, William."

He picked up the pace.

"Harder. Not faster."

"Yes, ma'am." He rutted his hips sending shivers through her body as he thumped against her g-spot. "I'm going to come."

Sparks of light burst behind her eyelids as her whole body tensed under him. "Don't... stop..."

His hips pistoned against hers as she sailed over the edge and into trembling bliss. A few thrusts later and he collapsed on top of her, her name roaring from his mouth. She'd never felt more beautiful, or powerful. She'd made him lose control, and the impression she got suggested that didn't happen often.

Something glimmered in her chest, the low flickering embers buried in her heart catching fuel and oxygen, causing a chain reaction of feelings and sensations that brought tears to her eyes.

Shit. Not only had she failed to avoid Will Morrison, but he'd fucked her even closer to falling for him than before.

Yeah. She was screwed.

It had been a week since she'd seen him. And when Will walked through the doors to the community center on the night of her fundraiser, looking like a model from the cover of a Billionaire romance, she almost peed herself. She rubbed her thighs together in a bid to get some friction for her insta-throbbing clit.

She wanted more. More sex, more orgasms, more lazy smiles and heated glances. More Will.

His hair was styled back from his face, his sharp jaw parallel to the crisp, starched white shirt peeking over the top of his tuxedo jacket. Bow tie... waistcoat... perfectly pressed dress pants, and shoes so shiny they could probably see them from space.

Fuck.

"Holy shit, they look good." Sabrina's shy giggle made her laugh and peruse the rest of the line of well-dressed hockey players making their way across the space toward her.

Oh, yeah. She was going to make a lot of money tonight, and she didn't care even a little bit that she felt like a hockey player pimp. She'd own that title. Hell, she'd get it tattooed across her forehead.

Looking as delectable as they did, she wouldn't be surprised if people thought she was a madam and they were her escorts.

On the ice, rugged, occasionally bleeding and toothless, hidden under padding and helmets, it was easy to forget just how fucking hot their team was.

Each of the guys wore a perfectly fitted tuxedo and smelled fucking delicious. Broad shoulders, strong jaws, and hockey butts she wanted to line up and take bites from, stretched as far as the eye could see. Why hadn't she brought a vibe in her purse?

"Quinny?"

"Hm?"

"I said where do you want Cleo to put them?"

Her eyes met Will's and he smirked. That lazy, crooked smile sent sparks of desire straight between her thighs. She cleared her throat as he stopped a few feet away.

"You boys sure do clean up nice." Cleo dusted the lapels of Linc's jacket, beaming up at him like he was the only man in the room.

Sabrina circled the desk they'd been sitting at and grabbed Russell's tie, shaking her head with a smile.

"Crooked?"

She nodded. "I got you."

He kissed her forehead.

Austin's girlfriend, Mackenzie, burst through the door behind them, bending to fix a strap on her shoe between shuffled steps. "Sorry I'm late!"

He grabbed her and kissed her unapologetically, with so much passion a few of the team cleared their throats and averted their eyes, but Quinn couldn't look away.

They'd all found their lobsters, the one person they were going to be with forever. Her heart squeezed as she turned to find Will's hot gaze still on her.

Sébastien stepped forward. "Where would you like us to sit?"

"Cleo's going to have you all follow her, we have seats placed for you guys to wait for the auction to start."

The players followed Cleo, but Will hung back.

"Penny for your thoughts?"

Quinn smiled. "Truthfully? I was thinking about how I wished I'd known you for prom." If she'd known Will back then, perhaps she wouldn't have gotten into the trouble that had ruined her relationship with her family.

"You better not let some old lady bid on me, Q."

He pulled her back to the present. She folded her arms and tapped her chin with the pad of her index finger. "What's in it for me?"

He buffed his nails on the front of his jacket. "You get to have dinner with me at the best Italian restaurant in town."

"I do love Olive Garden."

He snorted. "If we went to Olive Garden you'd never want to see me again. I can put away a shameful quantity of bread-sticks and alfredo sauce."

"I bet I'm worse."

"Challenge accepted." She jerked her chin. "Go. Before Cleo gets grumpy you left the pack. Is that what a group of hockey players in the wild is called?"

"Is the collective term a 'yum' of hockey players?."

Will's head snapped toward Pippa, the woman who ran the women's shelter.

"You must be Will." She flicked a cursory glance between Will and Quinn, making Quinn's cheeks flare. Pippa was the only family Quinn had left, it stood to reason she'd do every-thing in her power to embarrass the ever living shit out of her.

"I'm Pippa. I can't begin to tell you how grateful we are for what you and the other Snow Pirates are doing here tonight."

She turned to Quinn, bright eyed and a huge smile lighting up her face. "I've never seen so many people at one of our fundraisers. I mean, sure..." She shrugged. "They're a bunch of thirsty bitches who want to be wined and dined by a hockey hottie. But I'll take it as long as they brought thick wallets to pay for those thick thighs."

Quinn blurted out a laugh. "Pippa!"

Pippa wagged a finger. "Nuh uh. Nope. You knew what you were doing when you suggested this fundraiser to me." She rubbed her hands together. "We're going to bring in a lot of money." Her face softened. "You boys are going to help a lot of women and children, Will. We truly appreciate it."

Will swallowed hard, and something passed across his face that Quinn couldn't read. His parents were more blissfully in love than anyone she'd ever seen. It radiated from them like a beacon. Was there someone else in Will's life who'd experienced abuse who needed the sanctuary of a women's shelter?

A frown pinched her face as he tucked his hands in his pockets and rocked. "You're welcome." His cheeks darkened. "It's a great cause. We're only too glad to help."

Pippa sniffed and brushed under her left eye before giving a resolute nod. "Let's get this show on the road."

CHAPTER 6

Will

Will fucking hated people staring at him. He hated attention. That shit was for Finn, or Linc, or even Austin with his quiet confidence and ability to stand under a spotlight without flinching. Not for Will. Speaking of Finn, he was there too but it had been awkward AF when he arrived. He'd given Will a stiff nod hello and that was it. Maybe things were beyond repair after all.

His skin crawled as he stood on stage, willing his leg not to tremble or sweat to drip down his forehead.

Thank God he wore a jacket. He dreaded to think of the sweat patches spreading through his shirt.

On the ice, it was different. He had a goal, a purpose, laser sharp focus on getting the puck where it needed to be and protecting his brothers from the enemy. But being a piece of meat in what was essentially a market in front of a few hundred women – even for charity – made his stomach curdle.

He swallowed as he scanned the room. The rest of the players' girlfriends stood in a line against the wall on the left, but Quinn took center stage for the auction. Rows of seats filled the small space in the center of the room as Pippa talked about the charity and its importance.

A few players down from him, Finn made eyes at Molly in the audience. Her bright red lips were pulled into a huge smile. There wasn't a single woman in the room who was going to win a date with her man. Will's gaze landed on a face that made his stomach flop like he'd missed a step in a flight of stairs.

Bile fizzed in the back of his throat, and he curled his nails into his palms to ground himself as the eyes of a woman who boiled his blood met his.

She had the audacity to smile.

If things were better between him and Finn, he'd pull their code word for 'get me the fuck out of here' and Finn would rescue him.

At one time, at the slightest whisper of that code word, Finn would have pretended to pass out, or pull the fire alarm, strip naked and throw his undies into the spectators, whatever it took.

But not now.

He couldn't pull his gaze from the stranger still staring at him. She had been his English teacher in high school and had offered to help tutor him one-to-one with the only subject he had struggled with his whole life. His leg jittered as he fought to steady his breathing and keep his shit together.

At first it wasn't so bad. Accidental brushes of their thighs, or their hands touching as she sat close to him.

His heart thrashed around in his chest, in his ears, in his temples as though it had been let out of his rib cage and was searing a path through his body.

When she tried to kiss him, at first, she'd seemed remorseful and swore it would never happen again. But it did. She touched him again.

He gritted his teeth. He hadn't said anything at the time.

Teenage boys had fantasies about being touched by an older woman. He was already an outcast for his love of technology and gaming; he'd have been totally shunned if he'd complained that the hottest teacher in school had tried to sleep with him.

And what if she'd turned the tables and accused him of being the instigator? His future was too bright to risk a sexual assault claim, or even just embarrassing his parents. It had been safest to press it down, bury it, and not look back.

He blinked back tears at the memory of her tongue forcing its way into his mouth. The bidding had started, and thankfully, as team captain, Pippa wanted him to go last. Hopefully he could pull himself together enough to act like he was fine.

When everything with Molly had come to a head, he'd been forced to take a breath and examine his overbearing behavior during the years since the incidents with his teacher.

He needed help, he wanted help. He wanted to talk to a shrink about how every fiber of his being burned to protect his sister from the harsh reality of the world that when women wore suggestive clothing or behaved in a certain way, they were seen as being easy. How a short skirt and low cut top were seen by some as an invitation.

He'd been violated, fully dressed, geeky, with acne and greasy skin. He had no idea how someone had found him attractive enough to make a move on him.

Molly was a fierce, powerful, and breathtakingly beautiful woman who knew what she wanted and pursued it without apology. She could be seen by many as a target, and the older she got and the more comfortable with her sexuality she became, so did his desire to protect her from the potential assholes out there who might want to take advantage of her.

Like his English teacher had taken advantage of him.

Or worse.

He closed his eyes, his foot bounced on the stage as a bead of sweat made its way down the side of his neck. He needed air. To breathe. Space from the woman that shifted his entire trajectory. The woman who, as a teacher, should have protected him from predators, but instead, was one of them.

The line in front of him got shorter again. He wanted to scratch his skin off under her stare. Had she made moves on other people in his school? If he'd spoken up, could he have stopped her?

Guilt swirled in his stomach, threatening to bubble up into his throat. Fuck. Would she bid on him? How could he explain to Quinn, or the shelter that he didn't want to have dinner, or coffee, or even breathe the same air as the woman who had inappropriately touched him as a teenager?

The room grew small, his chest contracted, sounds amplified, and his head pounded so hard he might go deaf. His fists curled into balls at his sides, he was probably drawing blood from his nails digging into his palms but it was all that was grounding him from slinking to the floor and curling up into the fetal position.

His body jerked from the shallow breaths he sucked in through his nose, and when Quinn called him forward, he froze to the spot.

Concern pinched her brows as she beckoned him forward. The reassuring squeeze she gave his arm when he stepped beside her made his shoulders relax just enough to take in a full breath.

Pippa made the first bid, and Quinn's eyebrows jumped so high it would have been comical had he not been focused on the woman in the third row.

When she lifted her card to bid, his body tensed. No. She couldn't. Could she?

White noise filled his head as he stared at the placard in her hand. Pippa bid again. And again. Until that woman gave up and let her win. Fuck. His tight muscles loosened enough for him to suck in a full breath.

He could hardly believe it. He'd expected her to keep pushing until she'd won, but dinner with Pippa would be a mercy he couldn't put into words. He owed her.

Auction over, he turned to a still frowning Quinn. Pippa made her way onto the stage and enveloped her in a hug before she could voice the questions dancing in her eyes.

"I look forward to having dinner with you, Pippa. I can't wait to hear all about the shelter, and you and Quinn working together."

Pippa shook her head with a knowing smile. "Oh! It's not me you'll be having dinner with, Will. I won it for Quinn." She beamed like she was a criminal mastermind. He kind of wanted to kiss the older woman for playing matchmaker.

Quinn squeaked. Will mouthed 'thank you.'

"For me?"

"Yes, dear. All work and no play makes Quinn a dull woman. You need to get out and have some fun." She leaned closer to Quinn. "And the way that boy looks at you suggests he might have a couple of ideas about what kinda fun you could have."

Her stage whisper was terrible, and the exaggerated wink she gave Will made him smile on instinct while his insides still quivered and came down from the ordeal. He liked Pippa. She'd given him what he'd wanted without him having to open his mouth and find the words to ask someone he'd hurt to spend time with him.

Unclenching his fists he managed another shaky smile, warmth returning to his body. Quinn's head shook back and forth at a frantic pace. "I can't believe you bid on a hockey player for me."

"Bullshit. You totally can." Pippa bumped Quinn's shoulder with her own. "Enjoy it."

He'd make a donation to the shelter to thank Pippa and pay her back. She likely gave her all to the shelter and he didn't want her out of pocket. Not when he was the one who truly benefited from her actions.

The woman wasn't quitting. She had spunk and he liked it. And now she'd given him a gift, he was going to make sure his date with Quinn was the best date ever. She'd have no choice but to fall madly in love with him and realize he wasn't truly a dick, he just spoke before he thought a lot of the time.

He'd do better, be better. For Quinn, for Molly, for himself.

He still felt eyes on him. His fight or flight switch was firmly set to flight and he couldn't contain the nervous energy coursing through him as his leg jittered. The rest of the team were milling around Quinn's baked goods stand. It was emptying at an alarming rate, even though he'd never seen so many treats in one place. She'd definitely come prepared.

"Let's go mingle and make yummy noises while eating cupcakes so everyone wants one." Pippa led the way off the stage.

"So, since you make cupcakes, does that mean they're your favorite dessert?"

Quinn looked over her shoulders before shaking her head. "I feel like such a fraud. I mean, I like cupcakes. Don't get me wrong. Anyone who doesn't like cupcakes is a total sociopath. But my favorite dessert is apple pie."

"Mine too."

She stopped dead in her tracks and shook her head. "Don't lie to me, William."

His chest warmed as she waggled her finger at him. There she was. "I mean it. It's my favorite."

"Apple pie is literally no one's favorite dessert. It's like the plain Jane of desserts. Everyone wants something more exotic."

"The classics are the best." He itched to reach out and pull her to him, knowing that if she was in his arms he'd breathe easier.

On their way to the treats table, *she* intercepted him and Quinn, blocking their path with her sparkly dress, red nails, and the same perfume she'd worn when he was in high school. His throat closed in with the walls of the room as the space around him shrank. She had the nerve to beam at him and open her arms, hugging him like they were old friends.

He stiffened as she air kissed his cheeks.

"Will Morrison, it's been an age. How are you?" She turned to Pippa and Quinn. "I taught Will English in high school." The weight of her expectant stare pressed against his temples.

"I'm fine thanks. I—"

"I'm really sorry, but I need Will to help me get some more cupcakes from the car before everyone sees the emptying table and thinks we're sold out. I'm sure you understand." Quinn pressed her hand into the small of his back and pushed him forward.

With every step he took away from *her,* the knots in his chest and neck loosened a little more. Quinn guided him to a smaller room, away from the crowd and the noise, pulled out a chair, rubbed his back, and turned to leave.

Grabbing her arm, he shook his head, but couldn't find any words. He closed the door and leaned his forearms against it, head on his arms. He just needed a minute to breathe.

Quinn's presence was calming. She didn't step closer, didn't touch him; she just stood a few feet away, quietly waiting.

Eyes closed, he sucked in deep breaths. He imagined the air filling every space in his body, breathing looseness into his muscles and warmth into his veins. With every exhale, he imagined the tension and anxiety blowing away on the breeze.

He had no idea how long he stood there, but when he

turned to face Quinn, her eyes flickered back and forth between his.

"I'm okay."

Uncertainty rippled across her features, but she nodded. "Then let's get back out there. If you need to be saved again, just tug on your ear or something, okay?"

He laughed. "Deal. And... thank you."

"Any time."

She didn't push him for answers as they walked back to their friends. The crowd had largely cleared, Pippa called Quinn away to talk to some potential donors, and as far as he could tell, *she* was gone, too.

"Hey, you're almost all sold out." His voice almost sounded normal.

Sabrina and Cleo nodded. "We thought the table would be fine with one of us running it while Quinn was doing her stage thing. But..." Bre gestured to the almost empty table in front of her. "We got busy."

"Well, we did invite a bunch of always hungry hockey players to an event with the best baked treats in town."

"This is certainly true." Will surveyed what was left on the table. "Know what? I'm going to clear the rest of your inventory."

"What?" Bre's shriek drew looks from a couple of the team still milling around shoveling cake into their mouths.

"I'll take them over to the rink on the way home. They've got mites practice for the kids this evening." Mites were the kid's hockey club for 5-8 year olds.

Cleo clasped her chest. "That's adorable, Will. So sweet."

"Actually. Can I leave half here? Can you guys tell Pippa that they're for the women and kids at the shelter?"

He glanced over his shoulder. Quinn spoke with a smile on her face, her hands moving with a passion that seemed to thread through everything she did. "Don't tell her, okay? I don't want it to be a thing. Let me just do this nice thing and…" He shrugged.

Sabrina nodded. "I can do that. But she's going to want to know who cleared out her stall."

"The 'who' doesn't matter so much as the fact it's for a good cause. And she earned it. I'm going to take these over to the rink. I'll see you guys around, okay?"

He picked up the trays of cupcakes and made his way out to the car without looking back. Placing them onto the passenger seat, he grabbed the seatbelt and strapped them in. He didn't want his precious cargo to end up on the floor of his car – while he was sure the kids would still eat them, they deserved better, *she* deserved better.

He started the ignition, but couldn't bring himself to shift the car from park. His heart raced, and he broke out in a cold sweat as he flexed his fingers around the steering wheel.

Dropping his head onto his hands, he couldn't fight the panic welling in his chest, the shame stewing in his stomach, or the tears brimming behind his eyelids. So he just let them fall.

CHAPTER 7

Quinn

"Do you know what Will did with all those cupcakes the other night? I saw him talking to you before he left, but whatever he did with them, we didn't get any." Russ took a drink of water. He sat at their dining table having polished off a bowl of pasta and an even bigger bowl of fruit.

"I checked with damn near everyone on the team. No one got any. And I'm trying to decide if he needs a cupcake intervention. Like, does he have a problem? That was a lot of cupcakes."

"Will bought cupcakes?" Quinn nailed Sabrina with a glare. "You didn't mention it. And Russ, you sound terribly upset you didn't get any cupcakes. Did you not get any on the night?"

Bre snorted. "Oh, he had plenty on the night. I don't think Will is the one with Quinn-cake addiction. And as for Will? He wanted to remain anonymous." Her traitorous best friend shrugged. "I told him I'd keep his secret." It was her turn to pin Russell with a glare.

"Bubbles, next time you have a secret you need us to keep,

it might be a good idea to let me in on that fact. Maybe something subtle, like, oh, I dunno, 'Hey Russ, your team captain did something very sweet and didn't want any credit for it, could you keep your pie hole shut?'"

Quinn laughed. "That's definitely subtle. But why didn't he want credit?"

"I guess not every good deed needs to be bragged about and put on socials." Sabrina popped a raspberry into her mouth and chewed it.

"Well, now my question is the same as Russ's. What did he do with all the cupcakes?"

Sabrina squirmed in her chair.

"Spill it, Sharma."

Folding like a house of cards, she sighed. "He took half of them to the kids' hockey practice at the rink. And the other half..." She studied her hand, avoiding Quinn's stare no doubt. "Pippa took back to the shelter."

"Ughhhhhhhh." The force with which Bre dropped her head onto the table was impressive. Dishes clinked and silverware clattered.

Russ's gaze volleyed back and forth between the two women. "Okay wait." He placed both hands, palm down, onto the table. "Can someone tell me why Will buying a truckload of cupcakes and giving them away is a bad thing? It's for charity, right? I mean, he didn't let them go to waste or anything."

The only response Quinn could muster was a groan.

"She likes him." Sabrina was so fucking helpful when she wanted to be. Quinn was going to take the batteries out of Sabrina's toys. Or remove all the labels from the cans of food in their pantry.

"No shit. Tell me something we don't all already know."

Another groan.

"It means he's nice."

"I'm so fucking confused right now. Is nice bad? Don't women want nice?"

"Nice is good." Quinn's whiney voice made her cringe. Where was the strong, independent woman her mama raised to flip the bird at the patriarchy?

"Still not seeing a problem."

"She doesn't want to like him."

"Do you think he doesn't like you or something? 'Cause, I can confirm, dude's smitten."

Quinn smiled despite herself. "It's complicated."

"Aaaaaah. The shit with Molly. I can understand the hesitation. Truth be told, I wanted to rearrange his face for how he spoke to her. But I'm not sure there was any spite or malice there. I just don't know what his deal is." He chewed on a slice of apple from Sabrina's plate.

"That's what you mean by complicated, right? You don't know why someone so nice and easy going is so controlling and shamey over his sister being sexually overt." He fell quiet for a beat before his eyes flared wide. "Maybe he's gay?"

She bolted upright in her chair and shook her head. "I don't think he's gay."

Russ's head snapped toward her and he wiggled his eyebrows.

Fuck. She was on fire. Sabrina giggled and shook her head while Russ's intense gaze held her captive. "I can tell from the sizzling cheeks that you're pretty sure he's not gay."

She rolled her lips between her teeth and nodded.

Russ shrugged and stood from the table, collecting his dishes and walking them to the sink. "I still don't see what the problem is. Go for it."

"She's certainly going to *something*. He's taking her out tomorrow night. Her boss at the shelter bid on the date with him. For her." Sabrina crunched on an apple slice.

"And he's already arranged it? Keen. I like it. Good man, Will. Where are you going?"

"He hasn't said. Hey, can I have his number? To thank him for the cupcakes? I know he wanted to keep it a secret but it'll eat away at me until I say thank you."

Russ pulled out his phone and called out the number as she punched it into her cell. She said goodbye to him and Bre as they headed out to pick up Russ's daughter from his mom.

Plopping onto the sofa, she sighed. What did she even say to him? She typed out a message, erased it, typed it out again, erased it again and threw her phone across the couch.

Words were dumb. Boys were dumb. Feelings were dumb. Her vagina was dumb. Everything was dumb.

She hadn't talked to him since the fundraiser. He'd been so pale standing in the dim light of the office, barely standing as he leaned against the door. His body had been shaking, his skin ashen with a sheen of sweat visible under the lights.

He'd seemed off balance while he was on stage, stiff, serious, furious. Emotions had rolled off him in waves and while she didn't know him all that well, she knew enough to know that he was uncomfortable.

She'd thought it was stage fright at first, until the woman in the black, sparkly dress intercepted them on the way to the cupcake table. Will had frozen rigid. She wasn't sure he realized it or not, but he'd grabbed her hand, making her near shriek from the pinch.

Something about that woman unnerved him, so Quinn had wasted no time in stepping in to save him.

His behavior in the office, just the two of them, was anything but furious. Will was broken. And seeing him so wrought with raw emotion twisted something in her own chest. Keeping her distance and letting him process his pain had been hell. She'd wanted to embrace him, stroke his hair, hold him tight and tell him everything would be okay.

She wanted him to open up to her, to tell her whatever it was that had upset him so badly he'd needed to step away from the event to regroup and take a breath.

She had no idea what to say to him after that. She didn't want him to feel uncomfortable or feel as though he owed her an explanation. Sure, she was curious, but she didn't need to know his damage if he didn't want to share it with her. She didn't want to cause him any more pain.

Sighing, she stood and retrieved her phone.

> Quinn: Hey. So, Russ let it slip that you bought all my leftover cupcakes the other night. Bre said you didn't want to make a fuss, and I almost didn't message, but I wanted to say thank you. It means a lot – Quinn.

She hit send before she could change her mind.

> William: You're welcome.

She waited in case there was a follow up. In case he was one of those people who sent fifteen texts in quick succession to say what he could have said in just one. But nothing came.

After ten minutes she was still sitting, phone in hand, scrunched up nose, wondering what the hell she'd done wrong.

She was supposed to be seeing him in just over twenty-four hours. She had no idea where he was taking her, and by the cool brush off '*Thank you*' text, she wasn't even sure he wanted to see her at all.

Her stomach swirled. She'd been unfair to him. While he was definitely a jerk when it came to women, he was clearly going through something himself. Something not even his sister or teammates seemed to know about. Which meant he was alone in whatever he was facing.

Her heart sank. No one should be alone when facing something that made them hide from their friends to compose themselves at an event.

Clenching her teeth together, she wiggled her jaw back and forth. Should she bring it up on their date? Or keep holding space for him to process and perhaps tell her when he was ready? She didn't know how he ticked, but she knew she wanted to be there for him.

Whether he'd let her or not was an entirely different story.

The doorbell rang at 5.30PM on the nose. It had seemed a bit early for a date, but she wasn't busy and was shamelessly eager to see him so she'd gone with it. Pulling the door open, she sucked in a breath. Hot damn.

Somehow, casual Will Morrison was even hotter than in-a-tux Will Morrison. Jeans and a brown sweater that made his eyes glow, soft smile, and messy hair had her ovaries bursting into flames.

He'd texted her that morning. All he'd said was pick-up at 5.30PM. Maybe he was just a man of few words over text. Or maybe he was embarrassed at her having seen him upset at the event and didn't know how to act.

"Hey." While her voice came out light and breezy, her muscles were tense and coiled. Sure, the date was a set up – thank you Pippa – and sure, they'd already slept together, okay, a few times, but something within her was desperate for him to like her.

"Hey." He stepped forward and kissed her cheek. "You look beautiful."

He. Kissed. Her. Cheek. She was definitely a goner.

"Thanks, you too."

His lips twitched.

"I mean, you look handsome." Stop talking. She needed to shut her mouth and play mute. Pretend her throat hurt or she was losing her voice. She needed to stop letting words just fly out of her mouth like a babbling idiot.

Maybe it was him. Maybe his lips on her skin broke her filter and made her bumble and trip over her own brain.

It seemed legit.

"Thanks. You ready to go?"

She nodded. "I'll just grab my purse."

Out at the car, he held the door open for her as she slipped onto the cool leather seat.

Had she been transported into a romance novel? Guys weren't chivalrous anymore, right? At least not the ones she knew.

Sure, Linc was every bit the swoony romance hero to Cleo's Elizabeth Bennett. Russ was the grumpy protector to Sabrina's sunshine. Finn would ride naked into battle without a second thought to fight for Molly Morrison. And Austin was the sweetest, scariest mother fucker she'd ever met.

But it never happened to her. She never found the good guy. Her dating history had been anything but 'romance novel hero' quality. She struggled to think of a time when anyone held a door open for her, let alone waited patiently for her to get situated and put on her seatbelt before he closed the door and circled the car.

"You okay?"

Rolling her lips between her teeth, she nodded and willed the words in her brain not to tumble out of her mouth.

After a couple minutes driving in silence, she turned to watch him drive. He was focused, his lips pressed in a firm line as he watched the traffic through the front window.

"Thanks again for buying up all my cupcakes the other night. It was really kind of you."

His face softened. "I didn't want to make it a thing." He flicked on his turn signal. "But I feel like it's me who should be thanking you."

Pursing her lips, she looked from side to side. "You ate them all yourself, didn't you?"

He chuckled. "I didn't. But I could easily have done so. You're a very skilled baker, Quinn. I could eat treats from your kitchen every day."

It might not have been the best compliment to many people, but to her he'd hung the moon among the stars. Appreciating the one thing she loved doing more than anything was a big deal to her, so big, in fact, she wanted him to stop the car so she could plant herself in his lap and kiss him until they were both dizzy.

"I dropped some off at the hockey rink for the kids on the way home."

She stayed quiet, focusing on the edge of her cardigan, running her fingers along the soft wool as he spoke.

"Watching them practice tugged at something in my chest. And I started to wonder if maybe my life's calling was working with kids, y'know?"

The fierce blush in his cheeks was the single most adorable thing she'd ever seen.

"The next morning, their coach called me out of the blue. I guess he got my number from Coach Swift or something. He said they'd like some help training the mites. Just part time, volunteer stuff." He glanced over at her with a shy smile on his sexy-as-sin face. "For now."

"And how do you feel about that?" Her heart was racing. He'd been so sad when he'd told her that he couldn't figure out what his purpose in the world was. Perhaps he was starting to listen to his heart. Perhaps he could find his joy, like she'd found with baking.

"I'm... excited, nervous..." Another flick of his gaze in her direction had her reaching out to squeeze his hand in silent encouragement. "I feel like I have a lot to teach them, you know?"

She nodded. "You brought the first championship to the U in years, Will. I have no doubt you have a lot to offer coaching the next generation of NHL superstars."

Shaking his head, he hung a left and took them into the parking lot for the mall. Okay. While she hadn't expected to be wined and dined, going to the mall for a date wasn't exactly high on her list.

She schooled her face. Maybe there was something inside that he wanted her to see, or maybe it was a quick pit stop to pick something up.

As though he sensed her reticence, he picked up her hand and kissed the back of her knuckles. "Trust me."

He parked in front of the Barnes and Noble entrance to the mall. Her heart did a little flutter at the bookstore. She'd loved books for as long as she could remember, escaping into another world and reading about things she could only ever dream of experiencing. The throwback to their first encounter at Cleo's book signing wasn't lost on her. In fact, his thoughtfulness warmed her heart.

He opened the door and offered his hand to help her out. She smiled. She could definitely get used to the perfect gentleman who was guiding her away from his car.

Her heart sank as they passed the entrance for B&N. She'd hoped their date involved sniffing books. She wasn't the only person to enjoy sniffing books, but the idea that Will would indulge her bookworm crazy made her laugh.

He was so serious, and while he'd bought her books the

first time they'd met, he hadn't yet witnessed just how deep her book-boyfriend crazy ran.

He led her around the side of the mall, crossed the street and onto another, quieter street. Her pulse picked up again as they rounded the corner and one of her favorite independent bookstores *Bored and Bookless* came into view as they rounded the corner.

Maybe book-sniffing was in her future after all.

A line had formed outside the store: about a dozen people stood waiting, for what? But as Will guided her into the line, she took in the window display. Familiar black covers with hot hockey hunks were arranged in tall piles.

Her eyes widened at the sign. Mira Lyn Kelly, local hockey romance indie author was doing a reading and signing. Holy crap! She stood in line to meet one of her favorite romance authors. She snapped her head between the sign in the window and Will's face. His cheeks were red, his eyes fixed on the ground at their feet, and he'd tucked his hands into his jean pockets.

"William?"

"Yeah?"

She waited for him to meet her gaze. "Are we here to see Mira Lyn Kelly?"

His cheeks flushed even darker as he nodded. "At the Sugar Bean, while you were planning the fundraiser with Sabrina... you had one of her books next to you."

She had, but his attention to detail stirred something deep inside her. "I did."

"As luck would have it, I stopped by here the next day and saw the sign."

"And you just... picked up tickets? Even before the auction?"

He shrugged. "I tried, but they were sold out."

The line behind Will curled around the side of the building. Women clutching copies of Slayers hockey books to their chest as they chatted among themselves.

"Are we gatecrashing an author signing right now?" Her voice was a whisper, but the horrified look on his face confirmed he was way too much of a do-gooder to do anything of the sort. "How did you get tickets?"

"Russ's mom has contacts."

Warmth swelled in her chest. "Must be nice to have *contacts*."

He smiled and nodded. "He might be a grumpy douche, but he has the heart of a romantic."

He'd gotten the tickets before Pippa had bid on the date with him for her. She didn't know what to do with that. The line moved behind her and she grabbed his hand, squeezing it as she shrieked. It had to be the best date in the history of dates.

Once inside, she made her way straight to the check out, paid for one of Mira's books, and hopped in the line to meet the author. Butterflies wiggled in her tummy. The reading wasn't for another thirty minutes, and the cashier had said Mira would be signing books again after, so if she didn't get it signed beforehand, she wouldn't miss out.

She slid her hand into Will's and pulled him to her. "Thank you. This is..." She leaned around the person standing in front of her. Mira was laughing at something someone at the front of the line had said. "It's everything Will."

Emotion clogged her throat as he slipped his arm around her waist and squeezed. "You're welcome."

Twenty five minutes later, Quinn was the proud owner of a signed copy of *Dirty Groom*. Her face hurt from smiling and her heart was full. Will had snapped a dozen pictures of her while she spoke to Mira and he didn't seem at all impatient or regretful that he'd signed himself up to witness her squee-fest in all its glory.

She wasn't even embarrassed. They found seats and settled in to listen to Mira reading the first chapter from her book. Quinn rested her head on Will's shoulder and closed her eyes. What kind of man went to so much effort for a date? And how did she merge the slut-shaming Will with the book-enabler Will?

After the reading, the bookstore cleared out pretty quickly. Will jerked her back as she made her way to the door. "Didn't you want to look around and see if there was anything else you needed?"

Laughing, she shook her head. "I always need books. I'm like an orphanage for abandoned books."

He rolled his eyes. "They're hardly abandoned if they live in a bookstore."

"Ah." She held her finger up to him. "But they don't get sniffed regularly enough when they live in bookstores. When they come home with me they get read, read again, sniffed and stroked..."

Her face flared hotter the more words came out of her mouth. "I'm going to stop talking now."

"I think it's a noble cause. Wanting to rescue all the books of the world so you can take care of them. You're doing God's work."

"I know, right? That's what I keep saying. But Bre doesn't quite agree." She winced. "She tripped over a book stack last night. She's not very happy with my addiction right now."

"We can still look, if you wanted to. I'm not in a hurry."

This guy. This. Fucking. Guy.

"How about we get coffee and cake across the street? That'll save my wallet from another $100 book spend, and it'll save Sabrina from another middle-of-the-night book related injury."

"That sounds like a solid plan." He offered his arm and she slipped her hand through it.

A few minutes later, they sat at a two-seater table hidden in a corner of *Cool Beans*. It wasn't her favorite place to get coffee, but their hot chocolate was to die for, and they had apple danishes that made her heart happy.

"Hot chocolate and apple danish?" He pushed back from the table.

"I can get it."

He held up a hand, scowling. "You could, but you won't. Are you good with hot chocolate and an apple danish? Or have you found something even better on the menu in here?"

"There is no such item on the menu."

He nodded with a smug smile. "That's what I've found, too. I tried their strawberry danish once and had to buy two apple ones just to make up for the disappointment."

She laughed. "You're speaking my love language here, William."

While he was at the counter, she pulled out her phone and texted Sabrina.

> Quinn: You'll never guess where the date was.

> Quinn: Not ever.

> Sabrina: He took you to meet that hockey romance author you're obsessed with.

> Quinn: You knew?!?!?!?!

> Sabrina: I knew.

> Quinn: I'm going to have to find a new best friend.

> Sabrina: Hush. You love surprises. Are you back home?

> Quinn: At Cool Beans for hot chocolate.

Sabrina: I'm making kissy kissy noises at my phone right now.

Sabrina: It's Russ. I'm making kissy kissy noises too.

Quinn couldn't help but laugh.

Quinn: I hate you both.

Sabrina: Lies. See you later? Chicken casserole for dinner?

Quinn: You're too good to me.

"What's so funny?"

"Nothing." She took one of the overflowing mugs from Will's tray and placed it in front of him. When she'd emptied the tray, she tucked it down the side of his chair, next to his feet.

"What's your favorite kind of cupcake?" She was going to bake just for him. She would make him the most delicious cupcakes he'd ever had and get him hooked – on both the Quinncakes and her.

CHAPTER 8

Quinn

Opening the door to the hockey arena with cupcake laden trays was a little more complex than she'd anticipated. She stood, trays of lemon cupcakes with raspberry frosting in hand, facing the doors, wondering just how long it might take for someone to leave the building and help her out.

Usually she made a dozen here and there, so accessing where she was delivering them to was never really an issue.

Having gone a little nutso in the kitchen, she'd baked four dozen cupcakes. One for Will and two for the hockey team he was coaching and an extra dozen for the staff or people who happened to see her walk in with a tower of cupcakes. There was nothing worse than seeing people chow down on something delicious and wishing you could enjoy it too.

She'd come prepared, and if everyone didn't already love Coach Will for his kind heart and excellent coaching, bribing them with baked treats would seal the deal.

She'd also baked him one of her apple pies. If it was truly his favorite dessert, it would be a disservice for him not to try one fresh from her kitchen.

Okay, fine. She may have been over compensating for the fact she couldn't get his stricken face out of her mind and she wanted to do whatever she could to make him smile. If that meant shoveling an extra ten pounds of baked goodies around his waist, then so be it.

"Do you need a hand?" A warm, female voice made her start. "Either that or you're having an existential crisis just standing staring at the doors like you can't decide whether to go in or stay out."

She spun to face the owner of the voice. A woman in her thirties, messy bun, oversized glasses, yoga pants and giant sweater that came to her knees, and flats. This woman was Quinn's people.

In one hand she clasped a tray of four drinks in Starbucks cups, and in the other a Starbucks branded paper bag.

The stranger took one look at the stack of boxes in her arm and squealed. Honest-to-God shrieked with glee like some kind of happy banshee.

"You." She jabbed her finger at Quinn, a wide smile lighting up her face. "You're the woman who made the cupcakes last week."

Quinn's heart sped up, rattling against the bones in her chest. Guilty as charged.

"Y-yes, ma'am. I am."

"Do you have a store?"

Did she have a...? What was happening?

"My son – he's on the mites – *loved* your cupcakes. And from the tiny elf-sized bite I was allowed to have from the little Treat Terrorist, I have deduced your cupcakes are the best in the city." She patted her stomach. "And believe me. I've tried them all. I'd like to book you for his birthday party in two weeks."

Quinn's jaw dropped open. Someone wanted to *pay* her

for her creations? Surely not? She couldn't have thought they were good enough to pay for, right? RIGHT?

Tears welled in her eyes and panic flared in her gut. It should have been a good thing. It should have set her soul into the atmosphere.

But what if she was just being polite? There was no way Quinn's cakes were the best in the city.

What if the woman didn't get enough of her cupcake to taste it? What if she took an order and then fucked it up by ruining her son's birthday with sub-par cupcakes?

She shifted the boxes in her arms. "Uh... I... I don't have a store, no."

The mom rushed forward and jerked the door open for Quinn. "Go, go, before you drop those and I'm the big, bad mommy who ruined everyone's cupcakes. But we're not done with this conversation. I want your card!"

She made her way into the building, trying not to trip over her feet or her racing thoughts as she shuffled forward. As much as she loved to bake, baking cakes wasn't doing good. And the more time she spent on creating baked treats, the less time she was spending on doing something good. Like the shelter.

Her chest constricted. Every time she contemplated moving further with her baking, the same inner battle wreaked havoc with her mind and body. If she wasn't doing good with her baking, she was doing something bad, ergo *she* was bad for pursuing something she loved, rather than helping others.

Ugh. She knew on a core level that it wasn't that simple, or extreme, but that didn't stop her raging impostor syndrome convincing her she couldn't possibly prioritize what she loved and pursue a career in baking.

The mom was by her side, opening each door that led into the rink, chattering away to her about how all her other mom friends would love to hire her as well. The woman was basically turning into Quinn's pimp. The more she talked, the more sweat trickled down the back of Quinn's neck and the more freaked out she got at the idea of leveling up her hobby into a business.

"Think about it, yeah? I know so many moms and they would all love to have the best of the best for their kids' birthdays." She bumped shoulders with Quinn and tossed her a wink. "And a few of them are turning forty this year – what better way to commiserate than to treat yourself to cupcakes? I'm Nova."

Quinn couldn't help but laugh. Nova pulled a card from her pocket and tucked it into the front of Quinn's jeans. Nova was determined, she'd give her that.

"And I want you to keep in touch."

A few steps ahead, Russ and Linc turned to face them. Linc rushed forward and helped take some of the weight out of her arms.

"What are you two doing here?"

Two things happened at the same time. Both men turned a fierce red color, and they both spoke together.

"We wanted to come and support Will at his first game." Linc rubbed the back of his neck, but wouldn't meet her gaze.

"Sabrina told me you made a million cupcakes and I wasn't missing out."

She had to hand it to him, there was something endearing about Russ's zero-shits-given admission of the truth.

Linc elbowed Russ, whose own elbow flinched toward him, but he paused, his eyes widening at the boxes of cupcakes in Linc's arms.

"Saved by the snacks." Russell leaned over and examined the mini cakes through the clear pane on top of the box. "You didn't."

Quinn shuffled in place, her skin burning under Russ's piercing stare.

"Are those monkeys?" Linc had joined in the peering at the cupcakes. She'd made edible monkey cake toppers for each of the cupcakes.

Yeah. She'd maybe gone a little further than she needed to – and the raised brows of both Russ and Linc confirmed that fact.

Nova pushed forward for a look, too. Great. If the ground could open, swallow her and the fucking monkey cupcakes, that would be great.

"You made Monkey cupcakes?" The awe in Nova's voice made Quinn wince like nails down a chalkboard.

Quinn shrugged. "Well, yeah. I mean, the team's called the Powder Monkeys."

"And the frosting is red, white, and blue, just like their jerseys." Nova clutched her chest. "Your attention to detail is just..." She blew a chef's kiss and Quinn's inner cringe grew cringier.

She prayed for the six year olds on the ice behind Linc and Russ to burst into a brawl and distract from the discomfort of the praise over her efforts. Why was it so hard to accept the enjoyment of others over something she had created?

Behind Linc's head, the scoreboard read Powder Monkeys three to the Bat's one. Her heart fluttered. It was just a friendly game, nothing really riding on it. But she wanted Will to earn bragging rights from his first game – especially since two of his Snow Pirate brothers had shown up to watch.

Quinn gasped. "Did you bring the whole team? I don't have enough for a hungry college team."

Linc laughed and patted her arm. "We're not idiots, Quinn."

Russ snorted. "Fact. More Snow Pirates means less cupcakes for us."

She and Nova laughed and the buzzer sounded, indicating the end of the second period. Nova pointed at Quinn again.

"We're not done with our conversation, Quinn. Come sit with us during the third period."

"It's not a bad thing that people like your cupcakes, Quinn." Linc somehow read the room as he always did. "Isn't this what you wanted?"

"Bre says you'd like to open your own cupcakery one day." Russ was still eyeing the boxes in Linc's arms. "We want you to do Jude's party, too." He licked his lips.

"Basically we want to be able to drop in on you somewhere and throw money at you in exchange for these crack cupcakes." Linc shrugged. "Is that really too much to ask for?"

"Can you two go put those in the locker room? Make sure the pie is kept separate – that's just for Will." A rash of heat spread across her skin and Russ waggled his eyebrows.

"You're leaving?" Damn Linc and his mindreading ability.

"Yeah. I didn't arrange this with Will. I don't want him thinking... I don't want... I just."

"Breathe." Russ's snapped order made her suck in a breath.

"I don't want him to think I'm some kind of crazy stalker or invading his life or whatever. He likes his space."

Linc nodded. "But he also likes you. I think he'd want to say thanks for these." He bobbed the boxes in his hands. "Stick around, go talk to the moms up in the stands. You don't have to make any commitments, but listen to what they have to say, hear what they need, and then decide if you want to go forward with it."

She gnawed on the inside of her bottom lip. Was it so bad that she really wanted to see Will? If his friends were suggesting she stay, it was a good thing, right?

"Okay."

Both men smiled and Linc nodded again. "Good. Now go make friends with the moms of Minnesota."

She cast a wary glance behind her as she made her way to

the bottom of the steps leading to the stands. Linc jerked his chin, encouraging her forward. She could do this.

Less than a minute later, the teams returned to the ice and Quinn had finished half of the croissant Nova had given her when she'd taken her seat.

"Aren't you scared? I mean..." She gestured at the ice. "It's a pretty badass sport, and they're so... tiny."

"Every time they take to the ice." One of the other moms sipped her hot drink, her eyes never leaving the bench.

"But they make it as safe as possible for them." Another mom drained her Frappuccino. Who the hell drank freezing cold drinks in a freezing cold arena?

Will stood on the bench, hunched over, talking in the ear of one of the little kids. The kid's head bobbed enthusiastically as Will pointed over his shoulder out onto the ice.

Will made dark workout pants and a zipped jacket over a black t-shirt work for him. Was there anything he didn't look good in?

Nova elbowed her. "He's a cutie, huh?"

"Hm?"

"The new coach. He's a hottie, right?" She gave a dreamy sigh.

"He's too young for you," the mom sitting behind Nova chirped with a grin.

Nova waved a dismissive hand. "Details."

The mom behind her snorted.

"You're not that old. He's just graduated." She realized her mistake as soon as the words tumbled from her lips.

"You *know* him." Nova continued speaking after another painfully charged beat. "Of course you do. He's the reason you baked a bajillion beautiful monkey cupcakes." She clapped her hands together. "You're wooing that boy with baked treats. I approve."

Quinn shook her head. "I'm not... I mean..." She flapped

her hand at her face hoping to put out the sizzling fire that spread across her cheeks. Why did even the mere mention of Will Morrison turn her into a complete idiot with a fire engine red face?

Nova leaned closer. "You've already scored with him, haven't you?" She laughed as Quinn flapped harder. "Don't try to deny it. You don't need to. So, what's the problem?"

"The problem?" Quinn couldn't bring herself to turn to the nosy woman to her left.

"Is he your boyfriend?"

She barely shook her head.

"But you've already been biblical with him, haven't you?"

She didn't dare react.

"I knew it. He's handsome, great with kids, and you've already been to pound-town with him – which means he was either terrible in bed, or there's a problem."

She swallowed hard. "I don't know." Her voice was so low she barely heard it herself. "He's a private guy, kinda quiet, likes his space. I'm trying not to rush him."

"But you wanna date him?"

She sighed. Did she ever? The date at the bookstore sealed the deal. She'd gone home and written four pages in her journal about how amazing he was and how someday she wanted to have his babies. Yup. Like some freakin' obsessed high school kid, she'd let her inner helpless romantic spill out onto the pages of the leather-bound book that held all her secrets.

"I don't have the best luck with men."

A warm hand rubbed her back. "Oh honey. None of us do, until we find the one worth kissing all the frogs for."

Tears welled in Quinn's eyes. She'd once thought she'd found him. The one worth waiting for. But the morning two lines appeared on the pee stick and she'd told him she wasn't ready to have a baby, he'd lost his shit and left her.

How would Will have reacted to the same news? Would he have supported her right to choose? Or would he have pressured her to do what he wanted her to do, like Tom had done?

"I think he might be a keeper." Nova gestured her cup at the bench. "I mean, I don't know anything about him. But I've seen how he works with the kids, they all love him, and they're already improving through his coaching."

As though he could hear them talking about him or sense her stare, on cue, Will looked up into the stands and found her gaze.

He beamed at her, giving her a wave before turning his attention back to the team seated around him.

"Okay. That smile could light up the winter lights at the arboretum." She kicked back and took a sip from her paper cup. "I want an invite to the wedding, you hear me?"

Quinn laughed. Maybe things with Will could work after all. Maybe it was finally her turn to get the good guy.

CHAPTER 9

Will

Will stared in strained silence at Austin's frowning face like he was in a boardroom waiting for a CEO to make a huge decision rather than sitting in his friend's apartment.

Signs of Kenzie embedding herself more into his life flickered through Austin's minimalist home. The greens and neutral tones were interspersed with pops of bright colors, a pair of her boots lay in the corner next to Austin's sound bowl, and a mug had been abandoned on the coffee table. For Austin, all those little things were a huge fucking deal. Will couldn't help but smirk.

Austin clutched Will's proposal and his eyes raked back and forth over each line of detail he'd taken painstaking hours to research and write. In fact, he'd made two proposals. Austin held them both.

The first of the two was for the local Jr. hockey team, the First Mates. They were Midgets – a division in minor hockey for players aged fourteen through sixteen. They needed an influx of money to get themselves back up and running after a slew of poor management and coaching decisions had run them into the ground. The team generally fed into the University of Minnesota, the next generation of Snow Pirates, and they were struggling.

They needed help and Austin was the quickest and easiest person he could think of asking, but, as a Snow Pirate himself, he was invested in the team on a personal level as well.

The second proposition was something a bit more personal to Will, and yet, it wasn't for himself at all. "If there's anything in there that doesn't make sense or needs to be fleshed out, just let me know."

Austin's face didn't change, but it was the third time Will had interrupted his reading, so even his unflappable cool was probably verging on snapping. Will twisted his clammy hands together.

Why was he so nervous? Austin was his friend. If he thought the proposals were stupid, or pie-in-the-sky, he'd say as much. If he thought there was something to them, he'd say that as well.

Will's foot jiggled under the table as he waited. He tugged at the collar of his shirt like he was in a boardroom waiting for a CEO to make a huge decision.

"Does she know about this?"

He shook his head. "I didn't think there was a need to tell her until I had something a bit more concrete."

"She might not be happy that you went behind her back."

"I know." He picked up the protein shake Austin had made him and flicked his wrist, causing the thick, pink liquid to jiggle. "But I also don't think she'd push herself to take the step without prodding. If she's mad at me for that, then she's mad. But if it helps her reach her dreams then it's worth it."

The second proposal was for Austin's dad to give Quinn a start-up business loan. He had no doubt the man would want to talk to Quinn herself and get facts, figures, and test the merchandise before committing, but it was a start.

Will had scoured what felt like hundreds of business properties across the city and had found the perfect space for a cupcakery. It was a street facing property with an industrial kitchen, the rent was reasonable, and there was ample parking out front and there were no other baked goods sellers in the immediate vicinity.

Unless she had additional needs he was unaware of, it was perfect. Pride bubbled in his chest. He'd gone to visit the property, walked around the space imagining Quinn with flour streaked cheeks and her auburn hair piled high on her head.

"Both of these are great." Austin held on to the pages with one hand and sipped his protein shake with the other. "Truly. You did good work on them, Will. And they're exactly the kind of thing I want my dad to get more involved in. The grassroots stuff. The community level, you know?"

Will nodded, sipping on his drink, not daring to let himself hope that either proposal could end up coming to fruition.

"If he really wants me to join the family business, then he needs to take things like this seriously." He waved the papers. "Thanks for these, Will. I was at a loss for where to start. I note you have left the suggested head coach and coaching staff for the First Mates blank."

Another nod. "Yeah. I figure once the funding is secured, there'd be job postings and interviews to find the right people."

Austin stared at him for a long minute, his eyes narrowing, the cogs almost visibly turning in his brain. "I like both of them. You might want to talk to Quinn about this first so she doesn't get blindsided by an offer of a substantial amount of money from the Bank of Morgan though."

Will chuckled. "I can do that. Thanks, Austin. It really means a lot that you'd sit down with me and hear me out.

Coaching the Mites, even just for a week or two, it reminded me of where we all came from. The nostalgia was strong. I don't want to see the First Mates go down with the ship."

He snorted at his own joke, swirling his straw around the liquid in his glass. "It's important that kids have somewhere to feel like they belong. I don't know what would have become of me if I hadn't met Finn and fallen in with the cool kids. I was a nerdy, gangly, awkward and uncomfortable teen."

He gave a mirthless laugh. "Now I'm a nerdy, gangly, awkward and uncomfortable adult, but at least I have good people around me. People I wouldn't have met if it hadn't been for hockey."

Austin frowned at the page in front of him. Shit. Was something wrong with the figures? Will had checked everything three times over, until his eyes went blurry and his head ached. Surely he couldn't have made a mistake?

Austin turned around the sheet in his hand. The words *"Help after sexual assault"* were in bold across the paper.

His stomach dropped. Shit.

Austin's face softened. "Is there anything else you wish to discuss, Will?"

He barely shook his head in response. He'd been doing some research between drafting the proposals for Austin and somehow one of the pages he'd printed out to read must have gotten tangled up among the rest.

"The woman at the fundraiser?"

Will's eyebrows jolted up. How could Austin possibly know what happened? A faint buzzing in his ears grew louder.

"I may not say much, but I see everything. I saw you on stage when you found someone in the crowd who made you visibly distressed. When she raised her hand to bid for a date with you, it looked like you were going to be sick, and the relief on your face when Quinn's friend won was tangible."

He stared at the glass, jabbing at the remnants of his protein shake with his straw, but said nothing.

"When you stepped off stage and she blocked your path, I almost intervened, but Quinn beat me to it. Everything about your demeanor screamed trauma response."

He couldn't believe what he was hearing. Austin's perceptiveness was insane. How had he identified a trauma response so quickly? Unless... unless he'd been through trauma himself. He jerked his gaze up, but Austin shook his head.

"Not me. As a dominant, active in a public setting, however, I have seen more than my fair share of trauma responses. It amazes me how little attention people pay to even the most obvious of signs."

Austin tipped his glass and drank the last of his shake. "I watched Quinn lead you out of the room. When Linc came looking for you, I might have suggested you were engaged with Ms. Richards and they should leave you alone. I left it up to his imagination what you might be doing."

Will managed a smile. How had he gotten so lucky with such a good group of brothers around him?

"Does Finn know? Or your family?"

He dropped his gaze again and shook his head. "I wasn't sure it was all that big of a deal. But when things with Molly got out of hand and I became such an overprotective asshole, I had to sit down and take a look at myself."

"If you do not want to speak to your friends and family about it, I suggest you talk to someone. I can recommend a few names if you would like."

He raised a questioning brow at Austin.

"Again, not me. But I have made it my business to ensure I know who to call in case there is some form of emergency at Protocol while I am there, or, indeed, with one of my own submissives."

He shook his head. "You're so responsible."

"I have to be. A submissive puts their life into my hands, it is my responsibility to both treasure and nurture it and keep it safe." Austin pulled a pen from his jacket pocket and scribbled something onto the paper.

"Here are two names and numbers. I would suggest the first, partly because he is male and it might be easier to open up to someone who is not the same gender as your attacker."

His heart raced as he accepted the piece of paper from Austin.

"Do not worry. I won't tell anyone, and we never have to speak of this again if you don't want to. But I am here for you should you wish to."

He smiled at his friend's formal speech. It was as close as anyone had ever gotten to knowing the darkest moments of Will's past and Austin was talking like he was a doctor giving him a prostate exam.

"Thanks, Austin." He stood. "I'm not hugging you. But I am going to go and talk to Quinn about the money and the building. And I'm going to call your shrink friend."

At least, he was going to try.

"Hey." Quinn's pink cheeks and shy wave were adorable, like she was still nervous to be around him.

"Hey yourself."

She stood back, opening the door wider to let him into her apartment.

"Thanks for the cupcakes the other night. They were delicious." He patted his stomach, enjoying the darkening red in her cheeks. Her body was so responsive, she wore her heart, and everything she was feeling, right there on her sleeve.

Whether it was her pink cheeks, chewing the inside of her lip, or fiddling with the edges of her clothes, she was so easy to read, and he loved it.

"You're welcome." She led him into the kitchen, and he took a seat at the dining table.

"I hear you caused quite a stir among the Mite Moms."

She laughed, reaching into the cupboard for two glasses. "That Nova is really something. She's like a hurricane in a bottle. Once she knew who I was, there was no stopping her. She was like a dog with a freakin' bone. She wants me to make cupcakes for her kid's birthday. Then the other moms she sat with joined in too. They're pretty demanding when they want to be. Water?"

He nodded, but didn't want to interrupt her flow, so remained quiet.

"It was nice to be wanted like that, y'know? But I don't think I can be what they want me to be. They want something a lot more permanent, more commitment than I think I can agree to."

His heart stopped. Was she really questioning her dream now that people were starting to notice her talent? Ha. Wasn't that the very definition of impostor syndrome?

"Then you're probably not going to like what I've come to talk about."

Her brows jumped as she placed two glasses on the table between them. "I have some broccoli cheese soup with fresh crusty bread; I have chicken salad, and I have fruit. Does that sound okay?"

His stomach growled in response and she giggled.

"Seems like it gets the William Morrison stamp of approval."

"You didn't have to go to all this trouble just for me."

She stirred the soup on the stove and ladled it out into two bowls that were already sitting on the counter. "From the sounds of it I'm going to regret it after you tell me why you wanted to have lunch together. So you'd best enjoy it while you can."

He nodded, cradling the bowl of steaming green soup with both hands and placing it on the table in front of him. She sat across from him, scooped up a large mouthful of soup, and blew on it before taking a sip.

Her eyes met his over the top of her glasses. Her contacts provided a better view of her bright green eyes, but her glasses gave off the hot, nerdy vibe that set him alight. Her every move bewitched him.

She paused, spoon poised in front of her mouth. "What?"

"I just like watching you, that's all." He shook his head. "That sounded far creepier than I intended it to."

"It's okay. You're my creep so it's fine."

He was her creep. At least, he wanted to be. But he needed to show her some vulnerability, to let her in, before they could further explore whatever lay between them.

He cleared his throat. "I don't think I can eat until I mention this. And if you hate me, then that's fine, I'll step off. I'm aware this is a gross overstep of boundaries and—"

She held up a hand, silencing him. "Breathe."

He nodded through a breath. "Breathing."

"Whatever it is can't be all that bad."

"I did some research."

A stitch pinched her brows in a small frown.

"Available properties good for a potential cupcakery business." He held his breath and studied her face as she slowly lowered her spoon back into her bowl.

"I found the most perfect one. At least, I think it's perfect." He had to get all the words out before she exploded. He needed to tell her what he'd found, and done, and then she could dump his soup on his head for being a meddling jerk.

He slid the printout of the building across the table to her.

"It's got reasonable rent, it's easily accessible, it's not too far away, and it's not too big so you wouldn't be overcommitting."

Her face was unreadable as she scanned the page.

"And before you say anything about money, I have that covered too."

Her head jerked up, eyes wide, and he passed her the proposal he'd typed up for Austin and his father.

"Austin's dad gave him carte blanche with some of the company money to get him onboard with stepping into the family business. I mean, he can't just go around throwing money at people, but with a well presented argument... anyways. I gave him this proposal. He seems to think there might be something here. A start-up loan to help you get on your feet."

He picked up the spoon and swished it through the soup, unable to meet her striking stare or eat a single bite.

She stood up and opened the oven, pulling out a beautifully browned loaf. Grabbing a giant bread knife, butter from the fridge, and a chopping board, she turned and sat back at the table before slicing the bread. The perfect crunch of the crust cracking was quickly silenced by the fluffy, airy pillow of bread inside. His mouth watered.

"I think you should pursue your dream, Quinn. I think pieces of your heart are in every single cupcake you make. Those lemon raspberry cupcakes were the single most delicious thing I've ever had in my mouth." He paused and shook his head. "Okay, that's a lie. The second most delicious thing."

She squeaked, her eyes impossibly wide, probably at his implication that she tasted better than her cupcakes. Even her ears turned pink.

"You bake with such fierce passion, such perfection, that you can't not share that with the world. Do you know how happy you made those kids the other night? Seeing their logo, their team colors on those treats made their day."

Her jaw dropped, mouth hanging open just a little, but he kept talking.

"I know you're torn. I know you could do great, huge things for the women's shelter. And maybe you still can. Maybe you can do it part time. Or maybe you can still volunteer for the shelter on weekends. Or... I don't know, something."

He put the spoon down, momentum and determination to get her to see what he saw when he looked at her. "Oh! Maybe you can have a special daily cupcake and all the proceeds of that specific cupcake goes to the shelter? I don't know. Anyway. I think you could still do great and noble things if you went ahead with a bakery. There." He shrugged and sat back, not taking his eyes off her. "I've said my piece. You can kick my ass for overstepping the line, now."

Her eyes flicked between the pages spread out in front of her on the table and his face. Cheeks and ears pink, nibbling on her bottom lip, and the slightest of frowns pinching between her brows, she opened and closed her mouth twice, like she thought better about what she was going to say.

In the silence, he tried the soup, a shamefully loud moan falling from his lips as he savored the cheesy broccoli deliciousness. It seemed Quinn wasn't only a talented baker, she had wicked skills in the kitchen, period.

Picking up a slice of bread and a knife, he buttered the thick, still warm piece of carby goodness and dunked it into the soup. It was only when he'd taken a huge bite and spilled an inordinate amount of crumbs over himself and the table that Quinn spoke again.

"You know I'm not done with college, right? This is..." She brushed her palms back and forth over the pages. "It's a major commitment for someone so young."

He nodded. "I had anticipated you'd say that, but hear me out. I think if you open it soon and do it part time, you can place yourself in the local market so when you graduate you have an already established – and hungry – customer base."

She fell quiet again, but her pale skin and tense face betrayed her anxiety.

"I could help." He shrugged again as her head jerked up. He hadn't thought about it prior to the moment, but he didn't hate the idea either, especially if it meant she could continue her studies and pursue her dream. "I don't have a day job yet. You could do the baking part and I could do the selling. You could open the shop for a few hours every day and I could be there to handle that while you're in class."

Tears trickled down her cheeks as she sat back in her seat. Shit. He'd gone too far, hadn't he? He'd pushed her and upset her again. Fuck. The tracks down her cheeks splintered his heart.

He leapt off his chair and crouched next to her. "I'm sorry. It's too much, right?" He nodded. "Definitely too much." He reached to sweep the proposal pages away but her hand slammed on top of his, making him stop.

"It's a lot." She sniffed, and wiped the tears from her cheeks with the back of her hand. "But not too much. No one has ever... I guess I just..." She closed her eyes and huffed out a long and slow breath. "No one has ever believed in me like this before, not least of all myself. I've pushed down the notion that baking should or even could be a priority for me for such a long time that I'd almost accepted it would be a hobby forever. I'm going to need some time to process."

She slid her hand into his and stood, helping him to his feet as she rose. Something fluttered across her face, something genuine and warm. Turning, she didn't say a word as she tugged his arm, pulling him behind her as she walked.

She looked over her shoulder. Desire heated her gaze and her tongue snaked out to wet her bottom lip.

He wanted to nibble on her lip, hell, he wanted to do everything to her, every damn day. He'd never before met someone who made him want to put them first, who made him want to hold their hand for every tear and share in every smile. He'd follow her to the gates of hell without question, and when they got there, he wouldn't be surprised if she made the devil a good guy. It was just who she was.

CHAPTER 10
Quinn

On shaky legs, she walked him to her bedroom, their clasped hands hanging behind her. This wasn't a spur of the moment heated quickie in the alley behind the bar or in the back seat of her car. It was different. Something had shifted, changed, grown between them, something profound and deep and she wanted to show him just how much his time and dedication to helping her fulfill her dreams meant to her.

Standing next to her bed, she turned to face him. She was probably the hottest of hot messes; eyes red and puffy from her sniffling, runny nose, hair frizzy and unruly from the heat of cooking in the kitchen, but the way he looked at her suggested she was anything but.

His eyes drilled into hers as he took a step closer, brushing her cheek with the back of his knuckles. "I think I'm falling in love with you, Quinn."

A gasp froze in her chest. She couldn't breathe, move, or speak. He came closer still.

"I've never really been in love before." He kneaded at his

chest with a balled fist. "But I'm pretty sure this is what it feels like."

The vulnerability in his soft eyes, the hammering pulse at the base of his neck, the endearing way he held her gaze, searching, as if for validation or confirmation that she might feel something in return, made her weak.

He opened his mouth, his eyes welling with unshed tears, and his chest heaving. Was he going to share his suffering with her? Whatever had made him freak out at the charity event?

"I..." Scrunching his eyes shut, he shook his head. "I..."

She covered his lips with her finger, and when he opened his eyes again she shook her head. "It's okay."

Relief, comfort, pain, and a myriad of other emotions she couldn't place swirled in their golden depths.

"Whatever it is can wait until you're ready to talk to me about it, okay?"

He kissed her finger then his head bobbed up and down. "Thank you." His muscles softened, and his shoulders slid down from his ears.

Walking her fingers along the edge of his jaw, she heaved out a sigh. As curious as she was about what he needed to share with her, she didn't want to push him. If she knew anything about Will Morrison, it was that he didn't like to be rushed into something.

She dragged her fingers along the curve of his ear, down the side of his neck, and around the trim of his collar, not once taking her eyes from his. "I have feelings for you too, William."

His sharp intake of breath was almost inaudible.

"Deep, complicated, wild and messy feelings."

He brushed his nose along the side of hers.

"Love kinda feelings. I'm falling for you, too." She'd said it and there was no taking it back. If she was honest with herself, she didn't want to.

Something had sparked between them in that bookstore months ago.

Something intense, something that took her breath away, and the more time she spent with him, the more she realized it was something true.

She covered his lips with hers, already sliding her hands down his chest to the hem of his shirt and pushing it up his torso. She needed him naked. She needed to be inseparably close to him, their bodies stuck together, kissing each other so passionately that they didn't know if they were even breathing, yet somehow still taking in air.

He tugged his shirt over his head and dropped it onto the floor with a soft *poof*. Hands splayed over his abdomen, she skimmed them up to his shoulders, enjoying every ridge and plane of his body as they moved.

"You are unfairly delectable, William Morrison."

His low chuckle tossed fuel on her already sparking core. "I hope my six pack isn't the only reason you love me. Now that I'm not training with the team, and you're feeding me cupcakes... I'm undoubtedly going to gain a few pounds."

"It's not the only reason. I like that swirly thing you do with your tongue, too. And I can think of other ways to keep you in shape."

His face lit up in a full smile that made his eyes sparkle as she unbuttoned his pants and shucked them to the floor, leaving him in a pair of black boxer briefs. The V leading into his underwear made her mouth dry.

What was it about sex lines on a hot guy that made a woman lose her fucking mind? She didn't know, but her mind was definitely all-the-way lost. Fuck.

"You're eyeballing me like a piece of meat, Quinny."

"Yeah but you're like... the primest piece of meat." What even were words? She probably had drool on her chin, and she didn't even care. She'd seen him naked before, a night of feral fucking that left her achy for two days, but they'd never taken their time – and she wanted to savor every second, savor him, with her eyes, her hands, her tongue...

Dropping to her knees she looped her thumbs into the band of his boxer briefs and slid them down his thighs.

While he was average in size, she hadn't been left wanting any time they'd had sex. It was one of the many things she liked about him. He wasn't a towering jock with unachievable muscles carved from marble and an oversized cock. He was a regular guy with a regular sized dick who didn't aspire to be something he wasn't. And she kinda loved it.

Already well on his way to being painfully hard, a bead of precum glistened on the head. She wrapped both her hands around his shaft, and brought the tip of her tongue to it, enjoying the tiny shudder that rippled through him.

His eyes were on hers, watching her every move, and when she pumped her hands up and down his length, he groaned. Snaking her tongue around his tip, she savored every muscle twitch, the sound of his breath hitching, and his hands balling into fists at his sides.

As she bobbed her head up and down, alternating between sucking and swirling her tongue around him, she placed his hands onto her head and nodded, not breaking eye contact.

"You're sure?" A muscle in his cheek twitched as he got the words out through gritted teeth.

She hummed around his cock, nodding, and his grip on her tightened. His hips jerked, pistoning once, twice, as he fucked her mouth. Humming again, she let him take the lead, building up a rhythm as he slid in and out. Cupping his balls, she squeezed gently and his eyes rolled back in his head before fluttering closed.

"So. Close."

She sucked him off like it was an Olympic sport and the

reputation of the entire country rested on her performance. Once he had finished shooting jets of cum down her throat, she couldn't help but smile. He helped her to her feet and cupped her face with both hands.

"You're amazing." He leaned forward to kiss her but she stopped him with a flat palm against his face.

"Don't you want me to brush my teeth or something first?"

The frown and crazy eyes that appeared on his face would have been comical if she had time to examine it. He jerked her to him, sealing his mouth over hers and kissing her fiercely.

When he finally came up for air, he was hard again and his hard shaft pressed against her as she traced the lines of his face. "I guess you really liked that blowjob, huh?"

He gripped the bottom of her shirt and wrenched it over her head in one swift movement, the cool air kissing a sheet of goosebumps along her skin.

"I really did." His lips were on her collarbone before she could react. Dotting lines of tiny, feather light kisses alternated with little nibbles of his mouth and teeth. His hands worked her pants down her legs, as his lips and tongue burned a path down her body.

He circled her navel with his tongue, tickling, and she couldn't help but giggle. When he did it again, she yelped. "I'm ticklish!"

"I know. I enjoy making you squirm."

If she wasn't wet before, she certainly was now, as he quickly discovered when he ran his fingertips over the fabric of her underwear, drawing a moan from her. She rocked her hips, encouraging him to add more pressure, but he slid his fingers to the edge of the fabric, slipped them inside, and jerked her panties away from her body.

She sucked in a breath, his fingers unbearably close to where she needed them. Charged anticipation drained every ounce of oxygen from the room. All she could do was stare as he glided along her damp slit before dipping into her.

Shuddering, she gripped his shoulders to steady herself as he sank his fingers further inside, curling them to press against her front wall.

Her legs buckled. He stepped her back two feet before the edge of the bed caught the back of her legs and she crumpled onto the mattress. He didn't remove his hand, in fact, he somehow managed to get deeper as she landed, making her writhe against him.

Slipping his thumb through her wet folds, he sought out her aching clit. She wasn't generally quiet in bed, but something about Will's touch lighting her skin on fire drove her to moan and wail like a banshee, but she didn't give a shit.

As he applied pressure to her G-spot, he circled her bundle of nerves with the pad of his thumb. She fisted the quilt either side of her body as her ass cheeks ground against the bed, riding his hand. He eased off, skimming his free hand up her body and pinching her taut nipple between his finger and thumb and squeezing.

"William." The growl that broke out of her body surprised even herself. "I need more."

He grinned at her. "I love how responsive your whole body is to me." His thumb increased in speed as her breathing matched his pace. "Your toes curling as your heels dig into the bed."

She tried to relax her feet but it was fruitless.

"Your whole body turning pink the more turned on you get." He shoved her legs apart and dragged his tongue along the inside of her thigh.

"Your little whimpers and panting breaths when I get close to giving you what you need." He spread her lips with his fingers and blew on her clit. Fucking blew on it.

"W-William M-M-Morrison."

Another cool breeze gliding along her wet pussy made her smash her lips together and hum.

"You sound a little off kilter, Quinn. Is there something you need?"

"Yes." Her growl did little to make him acquiesce to her need.

"Tell me…" He blew on her again, pressing his fingers hard against her inside. "What do you need?"

Who knew William fucking Morrison was a goddamn tease in the bedroom? Certainly not Quinn, but next time she would make him pay for turning her into a soaking wet puddle of aching need.

His voice was low and gravelly, laden with lust. "Tell me what you need, Quinny. I'm only too happy to give it to you."

Under normal circumstances, she'd smack him for calling her Quinny. It wasn't the first time. Only Bre got to do that and only somet—Oh. Shit. His finger slid up and down her lips, but didn't dip between them. She arched her back. "Please, Will. Please make me come."

He didn't make her repeat herself before burying his face between her thighs and lapping at her clit with a hungry tongue. The way Will Morrison ate pussy was the way he seemingly faced everything in his life: determined, intense, and with a focused precision that had her at the edge in less than a minute.

Hissing out a breath she wiggled her hips. She wasn't generally easy to get off, but Will made it seem as though he had a cheat code to her orgasm and was thumping the buttons on her controller pad with his damn tongue.

"I'm… I'm close, William… I'm… gonna…"

A scream finished her sentence as she broke apart like a star going supernova, splintering into a million pieces as she came hard on his face. She would have been ashamed of herself too, but his satisfied hum sending tiny fissions and tremors through her body from her core settled her nerves.

"You're so beautiful when you come, Quinn."

His words alone almost made her do it again. He'd lifted his head just enough to speak, and rubbed his stubbly chin over her hood, dragging a moan from her.

Fisting the sheets, she writhed under his touch, wanting more – no, needing more. She needed him inside her, filling her, surrounding her with his scent, his protectiveness, and his deliciousness.

Aching need swept through her, deep, demanding, dangerous. "William... please... Get inside me." She bucked her hips to punctuate her words, but he was already sliding up her body, dotting kisses as he moved.

Her breathing turned to panting as he brushed his lips over her hard nipples, then along the lines of her collar bones. His hard cock pressed against her abdomen as she tipped her head away, granting him access to the column of her neck.

"William..." She'd beg if she had to. Her taut body yearned for him to slide inside, to give her what she craved. He pulled his hips back and angled himself so the tip of his dick slid through her soaking wet folds sending a shudder through her.

He leaned to the side, arm outstretched, but she stopped him. "I'm okay without a condom."

His brows flinched. "Are you sure?"

She nodded. "Birth control, and it's been..." Her whole body heated. "You're the only person I've been with in a long time."

Sliding her hands through his hair, she pulled him to her, hugging him against her. Her eyes rolled back in her head as he settled between her thighs and inched himself inside her a little at a time.

He hissed out a breath. "I've never been bare with anyone before you." Muscles twitched in his cheeks and jaw as he leaned on his elbows over her. "I don't wanna blow my load just from sinking into you, Quinn. But, fuck. Your perfect pussy makes it hard to resist coming on contact."

She couldn't help but giggle before clenching her muscles around him, enjoying the growly sound he made against her ear.

"You're so tight..." He moved back, pulling his cock from her before sliding back in. "So hot... so wet..." His eyes never left hers. He brushed the sweaty hair from her eyes and cradled her face like she was a precious stone.

She could get used to being looked at like that. Like she was an orange Starburst. Sure, most people preferred the pink or red, but her favorite was orange, and he looked at her like he'd just scored a bag of only orange Starburst candies, and he wasn't sharing.

"What?" He paused and dipped to drop a chaste kiss on her lips. "What's that face?"

She bit down on her lip and shook her head. No way.

"I'm going to get a complex about my dick if you don't tell me."

She couldn't quite tell if he was kidding or not so she huffed out a puff of air. "Nothing bad. You're just looking at me like you opened a bag of Starburst and found they're all your favorite flavor. I like it."

He kissed her again and time stopped, slow, deliberate, and so full of unspoken emotion it made her heart twitch.

He pulled back, brushing his nose against hers. "You are my favorite Starburst."

CHAPTER 11

Quinn

"Relax." Will's warm hand swept up and down her back as he led her up the front yard path to his childhood home.

"You know telling someone to relax doesn't actually increase their chances of relaxing, right?" She spoke out of the side of her mouth, not breaking the smile she held in place for Will's mom who stood in the doorway, a smile of her own lighting up her face.

"I'm not the one who's nervous, William. I feel like you might be deflecting."

He cleared his throat. "Is now a good time to tell you you're the first girl I've ever brought home?"

Holy cannoli! She was the first girl he'd brought home to his parents. And so soon after they'd gotten together, too. She wasn't sure if she should laugh, cry, scream, or some weird hybrid combination of all three.

While things were moving quickly between them, it wasn't too fast. At least, she didn't think so. But meeting the parents was always a big deal, not least of all when you were the first girlfriend they'd met.

She didn't have a stellar track record of meeting her boyfriend's parents. She'd done it twice before. The first time, she'd puked on their couch, and the second her boyfriend had confessed he'd cheated on her right before they went inside and she dumped a glass of iced tea over his head.

She could do this. She could absolutely meet Will's nice, normal, suburban parents. She'd heard through the grapevine that they were totally chill. Quinn just had to stay chill, too.

No pressure.

Mrs. Morrison ushered them inside and embraced Will. They were probably chatting, but Quinn's feet carried her around the living space. It wasn't small by any means, but it was as though someone had plucked their house out of a Steve Martin movie. Shelves with books and silver framed photographs of Will, Molly, and Finn lined the walls.

When she got close, she realized it wasn't just pictures of Will and Finn on the walls and furniture: Mrs. Morrison had pictures of every Pirate from their team. Her heart pinched. She didn't talk about her own family much. It wasn't that they didn't get along, but she came from a blue collar family. Her parents worked hard and expected Quinn to work hard, too.

And while she was sure they loved her, this overt expression... a near public display of Mrs. Morrison's love for her kids clogged her throat as she trailed her finger along the edge of the shelf.

She'd kill for her parents to be as invested in her life. If they were, perhaps she wouldn't feel so conflicted about where she wanted her life to go. A bitter taste rose in her mouth and she pushed it down. The room was quiet, had they moved into another one?

She turned to face them both. His mom's eyebrows were raised and a smile warmed Quinn's chest. Will's brows, on the other hand, were stitched together by a small frown. He canted his head, concern in his eyes.

Quinn's face was on fire. Laughing nervously, she shrugged. "Sorry. I..." She gestured around the room: clean but not pristine, lived in but not untidy, warm but not cluttered.

"You have a beautiful house here Mrs. Morrison. I can feel the love for your children radiating from every inch of this room." She rubbed her chest and blinked back tears. What the hell was wrong with her? She was acting like a fucking crazy person in front of her boyfriend's mom. "It's a little over-whelming."

Mrs. Morrison bolted forward and wrapped her in the hug to trump all hugs. Not that she should be surprised, Will gave pretty epic hugs, too. But it was as though Mrs. Mo was squeezing back together each and every broken shard within Quinn.

"Will's dad made ribs." Mrs. Mo spoke into Quinn's hair. "And I may or may not have made pie."

"Apple?" She gasped against Mrs. Morrison's shoulder which shook with laughter.

"Of course. Will's favorite."

She pulled out of the hug, fearful that if she stayed there much longer, she would make things weird, or worse, she'd never leave. "It's my favorite too."

Her heart soared. The love in the space around her was tangible. She'd heard about Will and Molly's parents from Sabrina and Cleo the few times they'd hung out together, but she'd remained convinced they were exaggerating.

As she inhaled the smell of books and good memories, a wave of nostalgia rolled through her. Will slipped his hand into hers and squeezed. He didn't say anything out loud, but his eyes spoke untold depths of concern, which only made her even more emotional.

Her family weren't local, she couldn't just call in to see them on a whim, but even if she could, she wouldn't want to.

She followed them both into the kitchen, sucking deep and steadying breaths into her body as she moved.

"Alex? Alex! Come in here and meet Quinn."

Quinn smoothed down the front of her skirt with sweaty palms as an older Will walked into the house from the backyard. His salt and pepper hair and the laughing lines around his eyes and mouth did little to hide the strong family resemblance.

Will had his father's eyes. The same, warm cognac eyes lit up as they landed on her. Alex stepped forward, arms outstretched, then paused. "You're a hugger, right? You're good with hugging?"

She laughed, nodding. "I'm good with hugs."

Alex swiped the back of his forearm across his forehead and exhaled loudly. "Phew. That coulda been awkward. We don't let our kids date anyone who isn't a hugger." He winked and pulled her in. "It's nice to meet you. Sorry we had to blindside you into coming to dinner."

He stepped back and jerked his chin to his wife. "But she's like a bloodhound, once she picked up your scent... well." He shrugged. "Basically you were screwed."

She couldn't help but laugh again as Will's mom tripped over her words in what appeared to be a bid to defend herself. "Will hasn't been home much lately." Concern furrowed her brow. "What with everything going on... I..."

She stopped herself, glancing back and forward between Quinn and Will as though there was some unspoken secret hanging heavily between them all in the room.

"Oh! I totally know about the Folly thing."

Alex's head canted. "Folly?"

"Finn and Molly." She widened her eyes. Will looked every bit as clueless as his parents. A blush raced up her neck and curled itself around her throat, settling onto her chest.

"Y'know... shipping? When you combine couple names? Cleo and Linc are Clinc."

She needed to stop talking. "Sabrina and Russell are Suss." Sweet baby Jesus in the manger someone needed to save her from herself.

"And Finn and Molly are Folly." Alex nodded like it made complete sense. Bless his cotton socks, she could kiss him. But she wouldn't, because, ew, and because, well, weird. She wasn't hot for her boyfriend's dad.

Mrs. M clapped her hands together. "Does that mean you're Quill? Or Winn?"

Quinn rolled her lips between her teeth and flared her nose. She hadn't thought about it, or the potential direction the conversation could shift before opening her mouth. Shit. Awkward, party of four.

"I prefer Quill, personally." Will's face was screwed up like he was putting real thought into the question and she couldn't help but laugh.

She nodded. "Quill it is."

"I'm going to check on the ribs. Take a seat, it shouldn't be too long. And I'm *definitely* shipping you two." He winked like he knew the best kept secret of the decade and left the kitchen.

Will's parents were so easy going, so warm and laid back that it made it hard not to feel like she'd been part of their family for years.

"As I was saying..." Mrs. M gestured at the dining table, urging her to sit. "Will hasn't been home since... well, the 'Folly incident,' I guess we'll call it." She cringed, Will cringed, and Quinn reached across the table to squeeze his hand.

"It can't have been easy for you. Finding out about them like that, or, I guess at all, really."

He shook his head, his shoulders curled forward. "I did not handle it well at all. I can't take the words back that I spat at Molly in anger." He swallowed, his Adam's apple bobbing. "But I can do better, *be* better going forward."

Mrs. M's face softened. "We can all only learn and grow, Will. I know things are still off between the three of you, but it will get better."

While he nodded, he didn't look convinced.

"Mrs. M, do you need a hand with anything? It all smells so good."

Mrs. M shook her head. "I got it. Thanks though. Do you want to tell me how you guys met? Will has kept very tight-lipped about the whole thing."

"We met at Cleo's first book signing. He walked right up to the counter, took my book stack out of my arms and paid for my books like some bookish enabling knight in shining armor." She laughed at the memory.

"We fell out of touch for a little while. Y'know... he was busy punching his friends and winning championships..." She waved a dismissive hand as Will choked on his water and his mom laughed.

"I like her." Mrs. Mo waved a spatula at her. "I like you, Quinn."

"Thanks. I like you, too. Our second meet cute was in a bar, far less romantic, but it led us here..." She shrugged again.

Alex burst into the kitchen with a plate of ribs in one hand and brisket in the other. Quinn's mouth watered. She was going to make quite the scene at the table shoveling piled-high plates of food in her mouth and she wasn't even a little embarrassed.

"Can you point me to the restroom please?"

Will told her where to find the bathroom as he helped his mom placing all the side dishes onto the counter next to the plates of meat. She could see why the Morrison's were famous within the Snow Pirates for their barbecue.

In the bathroom, she pulled up her shirt and snapped a

picture of her new bra. She'd seen a video on TikTok that made her snort soda out her nose and she wanted to try it herself.

Alex and Will were plating up when she got back into the kitchen. "Please ignore the terrible manners of the males of the household. They weren't – as might be assumed – raised by wolves. They're just getting hangry and need to be kept under control." Mrs. Mo handed her a plate and swept an arm toward the food.

Bacon wrapped asparagus, cheesy mashed potatoes, mac and cheese, corn on the cob, pasta salad, rainbow slaw, a green salad, and a bowl of his mom's famous watermelon and feta salad. She wiped her chin just in case her drool had made a bid for freedom. What. A. Spread.

There was no way one meal would be enough to wade through all of these culinary delights. She should have brought some Tupperware.

"I have plenty of Tupperware for you to borrow." Mrs. Mo scooped a pile of cheesy mash onto her plate. "Finding a matching lid might be somewhat problematic, but I feel like if we apply ourselves, we can make something work."

The words had escaped her lips, along with some drool. She wiped her mouth. "This is... wow. You really went to a lot of effort for just us." Her stomach growled loudly as if to hurry her along. She dumped sloppy spoonfuls of whatever she could fit on her plate before sitting next to Will.

"You didn't tell me your mom was going to so much trouble, William!" She picked up her phone. Her cheer-up-treat was now payback for him not better preparing her to meet his parents for dinner.

A text at 10.30AM asking her to dinner, followed by an 'it's with my parents' once she'd already said yes, was hardly fair. But she'd rolled with it. He hadn't even let her pick up a bottle of wine or a bunch of flowers on their way. He'd said he didn't want to set a precedent where he was tied to bringing stuff home for his mom every time he visited.

Regret curled in her stomach like lead. She should have trusted her gut and brought something, hell, she could even have baked something. Will's phone sat face-up on the table next to him as he shoveled food into his open mouth.

Was he even chewing before swallowing? His head was lowered over the plate, as though to shorten the distance the food had to travel to his mouth.

Her mouth hung open as she watched both Will and Alex cram an inhuman amount of food into their mouths. Will's mom stared at her with a small smile on her face.

She jerked a thumb at them. "Are they always like this?"

Mrs. M nodded. "When it's brisket time, there's no coming between the Morrison men and their meat."

Quinn hit send on the picture and tucked her phone into her butt pocket. Take *that* William Morrison. She couldn't help the smirk that spread across her face as she took an over-sized bite of the melt-in-your-mouth brisket and moaned, loudly.

In his defense, the brisket was probably worth the short notice, the lack of preparation, and the awkward nervousness of meeting your partner's parents, but he needed to let go a little and she was just the woman to help him.

Plus, she really loved her new Wonder Woman bra.

Groaning, she gave two thumbs up to Alex, not wanting to speak with her mouth full, then swallowed. "Mrs. Morrison, this watermelon salad totally lives up to the hype." She was going to have to take some of that with her and deconstruct it to make it herself. It was delicious.

"Please. Call me Erika."

She'd never heard any of her friends, or the players call Will's mom anything other than Mrs. Mo, or Mrs. M. It felt weird to be given her name, but she'd take it in stride.

Will's screen finally lit up with an incoming message. His mouth stopped moving and he canted his head, frowning. He glanced across the table at Quinn who pretended to be overly interested in her bacon wrapped asparagus. Was that parmesan sprinkled over it?

Hot damn, she'd never had a more delicious piece of asparagus in all her life. When she snuck a look over the rims of her glasses, Will had picked up his phone and was staring wide-eyed and open-mouthed.

Quinn schooled her face as Will's eyes burned holes into her. He coughed – more like he'd swallowed something down the wrong hole than the polite cough you'd use to get someone's attention.

"Will?" Concern furrowed Erika's brow. "You good?"

Quinn slipped her phone out and sent him the photo she'd taken of her matching boy shorts.

His eyebrows shot off his head and into outer space when the photo landed on his phone. She struggled to keep a straight face. His bugged out eyes made her giggle as she gnawed at the dripping with butter corn cob.

"Dare I ask?" Amusement danced in Erika's eyes. Alex was seemingly oblivious, or deliberately ignoring what was happening, and Will was, in fact, the color of a tomato.

He shook his head and downed half his glass of water. "It's nothing." He thumped at his chest with his fist, coughing. "All good." He flexed his watering eyes at Quinn before glancing back at the screen one last time, locking it and shoving it into his pocket.

She'd probably pay for it later, but his shoulders sank from his ears. He probably still felt some residual 'ick' between himself and his parents after Folly-gate. He hadn't been around much, Erika had said. She wanted to reach out and squish him, but she was afraid he'd react like a dog eating dinner and snap at her hands.

Erika met her eyes across the table and mouthed "thank you," twisting something in her chest. She took a bite of her corn and nodded.

"Tell me about yourself, Quinn. What do you study? Do you have a part time job? Tell me everything." Erika made her way to the oven and placed the apple pie in to heat.

Will rolled his eyes and smiled but somehow didn't stop chowing down on his overstuffed mouthful of food.

"I study gender, women, and sexuality studies."

Erika's lips twitched like she was fighting a smile and she looked at Will but said nothing, instead taking a bite from a rib.

"She also volunteers at the local women's shelter."

"Pippa's Place?"

Quinn dropped her fork with a clang. "You know Pippa?"

Erika nodded. "We went to school together. I'm one of her annual donors. Such a great cause."

Will paused, rib halfway to his mouth and swallowed whatever was already in there. "Did you know that women are assaulted, on average, thirty five times before they seek help?"

Quinn's eyes narrowed. Had he read their website? Pippa hadn't gone into that much detail at the fundraiser.

"I did. And something like one third of abuse starts during pregnancy. It's awful. Oh. Will was at a fundraiser for Pippa's Place recently..." She pointed the rib in her hand at Quinn. "That was you?"

She nodded. "Pippa bid on the date with Will for me. She waved that bidding card around like a demented cupid."

"Did you know that 81% of women and 43% of men report experiencing some form of sexual harassment and-or assault in their lifetime?" Will wouldn't meet her eyes, or drop the subject, but he'd stopped eating and was piercing a hole into his water glass with his glare.

"I didn't think it would be so high for men." Alex took a

long drink. "I can't imagine how hard it would be for a man to stand up and say he'd been assaulted. I wish society made it easier for male victims."

Wasn't that the truth? She'd always thought it was grossly unfair that society had sculpted men into these 'hard' beings who were somehow denied from having feelings, or expressing themselves.

"We have men in the shelter sometimes. Not many, but we do."

Erika nodded, Alex's eyes widened, and something flickered across Will's face that Quinn couldn't decipher. They continued to eat in silence until Quinn couldn't stuff another bite in her mouth.

Erika stood to rescue the apple pie from the oven and true to form, Quinn's dessert belly rumbled. "Oh, man. How did I forget about the pie?"

Will pushed the remnants of his mac and cheese around his plate, scowling at the fork in his hand. Whatever was going on with him, he clearly needed someone and *she* needed to find a way to let him know that she was that someone. He could trust her and let her in. She just had no idea how to get through to him.

CHAPTER 12

Will

"Do you want to come in?" Quinn draped an arm over the top of the door frame, leaning into the car. She clutched a bag stuffed with leftovers in her free hand. If anyone tried to take it from her, he was pretty sure she'd throw down. He was also pretty sure she'd end them.

As expected, she'd loved Mom's cooking, almost as much as Mom and Dad had loved Quinn. He'd enjoyed their meeting far more than he'd expected to. If it wasn't for the glaring absence of Finn and Molly at the table, it would have even felt normal.

"Will?"

He met her gaze. If he went inside with her, she'd undoubtedly quiz him about things getting dark and awkward at the table.

He tilted his head and studied her face, all soft lines and button nose. Was he ready to let her in? To tell her what happened to him all those years ago?

Shifting the car into park, he nodded. "Sure." His insides thrashed and his stomach threatened to expel Mom's watermelon salad – he probably should have stopped at two helpings but he couldn't ever help himself.

When they were out of the car, Will slid his hand onto the curve of her lower spine.

She tossed a shy smile over her shoulder. "I like when you do that."

"That's good, because I like doing it." He rubbed circles in the small of her back as she led the way up to her apartment.

He loved touching her. He loved the physical connection he'd never had before. Holding hands, interlocking pinky fingers, looping their arms together, brushing hair from her face... Having never allowed himself to get very close to people in the past, the tactile nature of his relationship with Quinn was everything.

"Sabrina is out with Russ and Jude." She unlocked their front door. "She's spending a lot of time over there lately. I feel like they might move in together." A dreamy sigh escaped her. "They're so perfect for each other. Even if Russ is a grumpy shit."

He couldn't help but laugh at her candor. Russ *was* a grumpy shit, but if Sabrina asked him to dress up like a unicorn and wander around town handing out candy, he'd do it for her.

"You want something to drink?"

He needed shots. Lots and lots of shots. But he didn't want to get fall-down-drunk and cry at her. Despite his choppy insides and the raging anxiety coursing through his frayed nerves, he asked for a beer.

She cocked her brow but didn't say anything. Beer in hand for him, and hard lemonade in hand for her, they made their way into the living room and sat two cushions apart on the couch.

He picked at the label on the bottle of his beer for a long minute before daring to meet her eyes. Concern, patience, and love. She wasn't hurrying him and for that he was eternally grateful.

"We don't have to talk if you're not ready, William."

The label on his bottle became interesting again. As he glided his thumbnail under the damp paper, he swallowed hard. She needed to know, and he needed to tell her. Keeping it inside as some festering dark secret hadn't done him any good.

It had made him an overprotective, overbearing asshole that no one understood and he hated it.

Maybe the old adage of a problem shared is a problem halved might be true. Maybe a problem halved could be a problem solved. Maybe sharing his trauma with Quinn would be enough to make him feel better, to lift the weight that had pressed on his chest, suffocating him for so long.

Her warm hand closed over his and squeezed. "I mean it. If you're not ready to share..." She shrugged. "I'm okay with that."

He shook his head. "I need to tell someone."

The frown pinching her forehead deepened as though she realized he hadn't told a single soul what he was about to tell her. "I'm here for you." She turned to face him, crossing her legs on the couch. Placing her hands in her lap, she fell silent.

He drained half the beer, smacked his lips, and placed the bottle next to the sofa. "Remind me about that, would you? I'm going to forget about it and kick it over." He laughed nervously, wiped his sweaty palms on his thighs and turned mirroring how Quinn was sitting.

"I was a freshman in high school." He paused and gave her a small smile. "Fourteen, almost fifteen I think. It was before Finn came to town."

Finn moving into the neighborhood had saved him. His racing mind charged ahead. He swallowed and brushed his palms along his thighs again.

"I've always been a science and math nerd." He shrugged. "I know. You're shocked."

Her giggle soothed something in his chest, encouraging him to keep going.

"I struggled with English. Subtext isn't my jam. Deciphering what poets and authors meant versus what they actually wrote... coming up with my own stories... reading fiction... It was all hard for me from a young age. And don't get me started on Shakespeare and Chaucer – ye oldey English... Pshhhh." He hissed and sailed his hand over his head.

He sucked in a steadying breath, but it did little to actually steady him. "Ms. Phillips was my English teacher, and she offered to help me untangle the knot of words on the page to keep my grade up."

Raking a hand through his hair, he shook his head. "As a straight-A student from the day I was born, it was impossibly hard for me to admit I was having issues, or needed any kind of help. Hell, I graduated top of my pre-K class with 'I didn't bite a single person' honors."

Instead of laughing, or smiling, her frown deepened. Obviously deflecting with humor concerned her, but it was actually helping him get the story out so he kept going. "The first session or two were largely fine. I mean, she sat a little too close for my liking, but we were reading passages together and answering questions so it made sense..."

A muscle in Quinn's jaw flexed, and her mouth set in a grim line. She knew what was coming, but she didn't stop him from speaking.

"And she was a beautiful woman, right? What kind of high school boy would I have been if I hadn't enjoyed the fact she sat pressed up against me?" He shuddered.

The magnolia walls of Quinn's living room inched toward him. Photos of Quinn and Sabrina hung on two of the four walls, looming. A large, solid wood bookcase stood against the third and where the fourth wall should be, an open space led into the kitchen.

He stroked his thumb over the soft brown leather of the couch, not daring to risk a glance at her. He couldn't afford to break down until all the words were out.

"But after those first couple classes, things got kinda weird. She kissed me at the third session." He trailed his fingers across his lips like he could somehow still feel her lips against his after all that time. "Then she brushed it off. Apologized profusely. Acknowledged it was inappropriate and promised it wouldn't happen again."

"But it did." It wasn't a question. Quinn moved her hand to his knee and squeezed, but she fell quiet again.

The silence was too heavy, too suffocating, pressing in on him from every side, so he swallowed down the imaginary ball of foam in his mouth. "Long story short, she tried to do things to me, encouraged me to do things to her. Things I didn't want to do." Acid burned at the back of his throat and tears welled in his eyes.

Forcing out a breath, he needed to speak the words out loud. He needed to take away the woman's power over him and shine light into the darkness. "She assaulted me, Quinn. She was supposed to protect me and she didn't. I was just a kid." He shivered. "She didn't rape me... but..."

Quinn cleared her throat. "Hey, no. Don't do that. Don't downplay your situation just because it wasn't 'worse,' or wasn't what someone else went through." Her voice cracked. She sniffed and wiped her cheeks.

Her eyes were red-rimmed and tears flowed freely down her face. "It's not a competition. Your experience isn't negated because it 'wasn't as bad' as someone else's, do you hear me?"

He hadn't considered that before. But she wasn't wrong. He nodded.

She shuffled toward him, picking up both his hands and cradling them in hers. "Why didn't you tell anyone?"

"Shame. Embarrassment. I was already a social outcast for being a hardcore geek. I'd heard some of my classmates bragging about feeling her boobs and doing things with her like it was the coolest thing. I felt like I couldn't speak up." He shrugged but wished he could go back to his younger self and tell him he needed to find his voice.

"But your parents... they're so supportive. They'd have burned the world down to protect you. You didn't even tell them? Weren't there signs of trauma? Didn't your grades drop? Mood swings? There would have been something..."

Her shoulders heaved from the huge breath she sucked in. "There should have been something."

He shook his head. "I threw myself into studying. I over achieved, worked harder. My grades were better than ever. Then I met Finn." He swallowed. "Finn saved me. We hung out every day and while he had no idea what I'd gone through before I met him... I dunno, I guess we saved each other."

He picked at a loose thread in the couch. "He has no idea what I was going through... no idea what happened... no idea how badly I needed him when he came into my life."

"And when Molly and Finn got together, you felt like you were losing your anchor, your person?"

He couldn't speak over the emotion swelling in his throat.

Quinn gnawed on her lip and narrowed her eyes. "And the woman at the gala? That was her? That was Ms. Phillips?"

He nodded.

"I knew I should have punched that bitch."

He chuckled.

She held up a hand. "Sorry. I just... I felt like something was off with her, like she was trying too hard."

"I need to thank you."

She reached over and covered his mouth with four fingers

and shook her head, scowling. "Don't you freakin' dare. If you're about to thank me for being there for you or for giving you space to work through your feelings, I will punch you, William Morrison."

"I mean it." His lips moved against her hand. "You steered me to a quiet place, let me have my freak out, and calm down without judgment or questions. It meant the world to me." His voice cracked, and his head pounded. Exhaustion weaved its way into every muscle in his body.

She cleared her throat, moving her hand back to his. "I haven't had an experience like yours. But I have a friend who was assaulted, so I do kind of get it. A little. I mean, I don't, obviously, because I'm not a victim, but..." She huffed and shook her head before sucking in a deep breath.

"It's why I volunteer for the shelter. The guy who assaulted her was never charged. She wore a short skirt, she'd had a few to drink, it was his word against hers..."

His chest tightened. How anyone could sexually violate another human being was beyond him. He shuddered. It was disgusting.

"It almost destroyed her. She fell to pieces. Couldn't sleep, couldn't eat, couldn't go out for a very long time. Her friendships suffered. Her grades suffered." Quinn's face softened. "I can't believe you went through all of that alone, not even telling your parents, and you kept your shit together the whole time."

She shook her head. "Do you have any idea how strong you are, William?"

He couldn't look at her. If he did, the years of emotion scrambling and clawing up inside his body would break free, and he'd melt down. He didn't want to break down. He wanted to be strong. He *needed* to be strong. He was the responsible one. The quiet, studious, straight-A student.

Finn and Molly were the trouble making kids. When Finn

had first moved to the neighborhood, he'd gotten into all kinds of fights. With his mom in treatment and his dad drowning at the bottom of the bottle, Mom and Dad had been the responsible adults hauled into the principal's office.

And Molly… she had been busted sneaking out more times than Will could remember.

He'd never been a day of trouble to his friends or family in his entire life. He was the reliable one. The one who gave out advice. He was a shoulder for them to lean on when they needed it – but he never took solace from them in return.

His jaw trembled and he blinked back the unrelenting tears.

Quinn opened her arms and legs, inviting him across the sofa, her eyes reflecting his pain, and her own tears trickling down her face.

He couldn't slam the door on what he'd just shared with her. He couldn't bury it again. It was out in the open between them. The cracks in his heart had deepened, and the pain and anger he'd pressed down for so long hissed and fizzed in his chest.

She beckoned him toward her with a wave of her hand and hot, thick tears were already coursing down his face when he buried his nose in her shoulder.

Warm arms engulfed him, coiling tightly around his shoulders as she held him. She didn't shush him, she didn't try to speak, she just held him while he cried and let almost a decade of emotions wash over him.

When the sobs racking his body eventually subsided into whimpers and sniffles, she held him still, stroking the side of his face and kissing his head through his hair.

❄

He must have fallen asleep, because when he woke, he was still sprawled out on Quinn on the sofa, and Will and Grace played softly on the TV.

Tipping his head, he brushed his lips across her cheek. "What time is it?"

She picked up her phone, lighting up the screen. "Two in the morning."

"Why aren't you sleeping?"

She shrugged. "Couldn't sleep."

He narrowed his eyes in the dim light of the screen. "Cause you had a hockey player sleeping on you?"

"Actually, that's pretty effective for my anxiety, it's like a human version of a weighted blanket. I kinda dig it. But no. I wanted to be here for you if you woke up. I didn't want you waking up and fleeing without me knowing about it."

She pinned him with a knowing stare. "It's common for..." She cleared her throat. "What you shared was a big deal. You've kept it to yourself for so long that it's only natural you might freak out about having said it aloud after all this time. I didn't want you bolting."

His chest ached at how considerate she'd been. While part of it was undoubtedly from her training and experiences at the shelter, the other part, the bigger part, was just her kind spirit.

He pushed up to sitting, and she sat as well, stretching both arms over her head. "It's late. Come lie down with me. You need to rest. We can figure out what to do next in the morning."

We. How could a single word carry such weight? Something twisted in his chest as he stood and followed her to her room.

"I don't have clothes... a toothbrush..."

She held up a hand, silencing him. "Sabrina said Russ has some clothes in her room, and we have a few spare toothbrushes under the sink." She spun to face him. "You can't escape, William, you're stuck with me. No matter what excuses you come up with, I can bat them away like Wonder Woman."

She picked up her shirt and flashed her bra. "I like the idea of my boobs deflecting away life's problems like Gal Gadot's bracers."

He couldn't help but smile at her obvious attempts to cheer him up.

"Let's grab some water." She made her way into the kitchen. "If you're hungry, I can throw together something before we lie down. I'm not sharing your mom's leftovers, obviously, but I can make you something."

His stomach sloshed, and growled, but he was sure if he tried to eat, he'd end up puking. He shook his head. "Nauseous."

She nodded like she expected his answer and turned to fill two glasses with cold water.

"I feel bad." He rubbed his stomach.

"The bathroom's right there if you think you're going to be sick. Though it would be a damned shame not to keep down that brisket your dad cooked."

He managed a small smile but shook his head. "I mean... I know she did things to other guys. And sure, some of them liked the attention, wanted it even, but..." His pulse quickened and he gripped the edge of the table.

"What if she hurt kids who couldn't speak up either? What if..." He swallowed, but the lump in his throat didn't clear. Blinking back tears, his knuckles turned white as he held onto the wood. "What if my silence enabled her to hurt other kids?"

A new wave of grief crashed into him as his legs wobbled underneath him. She abandoned the glasses of water and rushed to him, banding her arms around his waist and supporting him.

"It's my fault, Quinn. I should have found the courage to speak out. My cowardice probably resulted in other kids..." He couldn't finish his sentence. His words had dissolved into the caustic burn racing through his body.

"Hey. Hey..." She grabbed his chin and jerked his face so he'd look at her. "No. You do not get to blame yourself, do you hear me? This is on her. She was the grown-up. She should have known better. You were just a scared little boy and none of this is on your shoulders."

She cradled his head against her chest as a new wave of sobs clattered through him. He could barely stand. Everything hurt, especially his insides, and he had no idea how to make it stop.

Guilt, shame, and a bone-deep ache for her other possible victims made him weak all over. Quinn slipped her arm through his, supporting his lower back, and led him to the bedroom.

He dropped onto the edge of the bed and she helped him undress to his boxer briefs. She stood while he shuffled into her bed then returned to the kitchen to grab the waters. When she got back, she made him sip some water before crawling into bed next to him and holding him all over again.

His body was drained of all energy. His muscles ached with tension and exhaustion. His stomach hurt, his heart burned, and his mind raced.

"Shhhhhhh..." The warmth of her hand against his face as she stroked brought comfort somewhere deep inside of him. "It's all going to be okay." Her fingers trailed a featherlight path up and down his cheek. "I've got you. You're safe. You can go to sleep. I'll be here in the morning."

Her calm, quiet voice repeated as her fingers traced lines over his skin. He matched his breathing to hers, eventually finding a slow, steady, and deep rhythm as her chest rose and fell under his cheek. She was right, he couldn't fight his demons unrested. He needed sleep.

He closed his eyes and let her voice lull him into unconsciousness, hoping that when he woke up again, he'd have a better grip on the raging battle of emotions roiling in his chest.

CHAPTER 13

Quinn

Quinn shifted the strap on her shoulder as she walked. Butterflies warred in her stomach. Maybe not butterflies. Hornets? Bees? Maybe crows... or seagulls – those motherfuckers were savage. Something big and aggressive and sharp or stingy. Something that made her queasy as she walked toward Will.

She wasn't sure how he was going to react to their conversation. A few days had passed since they'd spoken, she'd come up with a game plan, picked up leaflets, and had a slew of support numbers written down for him.

Austin had already given him numbers for two psychologists, but the numbers she'd gathered for him were for various support groups and survivors of assault.

She just needed to present it all to him. She needed to let him know there were people out there who could help, and encourage him to speak up about his experience. The longer she stewed things over, the more she realized that woman, that teacher, Ms. Phillips, needed to be stopped.

If not solely to get justice for her existing victims, but because neither she nor Will knew with any level of certainty that his abuser wasn't still hurting children. Quinn shuddered. She wanted to rip the woman's head from her shoulders.

As she approached, Will's warm and nervous smile eased her frayed nerves. He'd know she loved him and was only trying to help, right?

She patted her stomach in an attempt to calm the flappy birds contained within, but they just squawked and flapped harder.

Ugh. She shouldn't have had that third slice of his mom's pie for breakfast. Erika had given her one to take home, and, loathe as she was to admit it, Erika's apple pie might be better than her own.

"You okay? You look like you might hurl." Will caressed her cheek, his scent invading her nose.

"I ate three slices of your mom's apple pie for breakfast. The only reason I stopped is 'cause I ran out of pie."

He chuckled. "She was talking about having us over once a month for dinner or something, just to catch up."

Quinn waved a hand. "I can't. I'd gain so much weight and end up fighting with Bre because I wouldn't share the leftovers with her. I almost stabbed her with a fork this morning when she tried to take a bite of my pie."

His quiet chuckle grew into a laugh. "You're not even kidding, are you?"

She shook her head. "It's a compulsion. I feel like your mom must put crack or something in her food. I almost went back on my way here, just to see if she had anything left."

"She's pretty great in the kitchen."

"She is. I might need to take up exercise" – she shuddered – "if we're going to increase our visits to your parentals. Should we go in?" She gestured to the building over his shoulder.

They'd met outside the library. Quinn had discovered a quiet space on the third floor that always seemed empty. That probably meant it was haunted by a bunch of unruly ghosts but the dead had never scared her, so she didn't give a crap.

Will folded his fingers over hers as they made their way up the stairs.

"Are you going to the rink later?"

He shook his head but didn't look at her as he climbed.

No spoken answer, either. Hm. Well, she'd already potentially upset him mentioning hockey practice, so it was only right that she double down and upset him even more by mentioning his sexual assault, right?

She sighed as he pulled the door to the third floor open. A small table wedged between two chairs was crammed into an abandoned corner. It was always cold, so she'd brought a sweater tucked over the bag hanging from her shoulder.

He pulled her chair out and waited for her to sit before sitting down.

"Can we talk first?" She twisted the strap of her bag in her hands.

His eyes narrowed. "Sure." He leaned back in his chair but folded his arms.

Not a good start. Defensive. Protective. And coupled with the scowl on his face, almost aggressive even. She needed to tread carefully.

"I... I picked up some resources from the shelter for you." She opened the flap of her messenger bag and rifled through the main compartment for the flyers she'd grabbed.

Placing them on the table in front of her, she steeled herself. Palms facing down, she put both hands on top of the small stack. "I think you should consider reporting that woman. Or at the very least talking to a therapist. Maybe even telling your parents... and Finn and Molly."

If he was pissed before, he was furious now. He pushed his seat back even further, and the vein in his neck protruded. His scowl deepened, too.

"I know you probably don't want to make a thing of it, and I know it's not my place. It probably feels a little intrusive."

He didn't speak but arched an eyebrow.

Fine. More than a little intrusive. "But you might want to give some thought to opening up to someone professional. It could help you process everything you're feeling. I mean... I'm happy to listen, and my training helps a little but I'm not a psychologist. It's not something I'm qualified to help you work through, and I think it could help."

She slid the pages across the table to him. "I know you're big into your research, and you like to be well-informed." Her heart raced.

She was doing the right thing. She was only trying to help. Sure he was going to react somewhat defensively, this was all fairly new to him. She just needed to say her piece so he could process.

"Anyway. Here. You might find something useful in these."

She held her breath as he accepted the papers and shuffled through them, giving them a quick once over. His face relaxed, and he gave her a small smile. "Thank you. This was very thoughtful of you, Quinny. I appreciate it."

He tucked the pamphlets into his bag and patted it. "I'll take a better look later." His phone lit up on the table. "That's Austin. I'm gonna slip out and take it, okay? I'll be back."

She nodded, gnawing on a jagged cuticle as she watched the rain beat down on the high window, heavy, thick droplets sliding down the pane of glass. If nothing else, the rain would keep him from fleeing.

She pulled out her textbook for her Women Write the World class and tapped her pen on the cover. She was right. She *was*. The woman who assaulted Will was a monster and needed to be stopped, punished, and her victims needed justice.

She tapped her pen harder as righteous indignation bubbled up into her chest. How could grown-ups be so shitty to children?

She didn't have an answer to her own question, but she wouldn't let it drop. She'd advocate for Will until he felt strong enough to advocate for himself.

"You wanna tell me what's going on with you?" Sabrina pointed a tortilla chip coated with queso and guacamole at her. "You have sad face."

"I'm okay."

"Will stuff?" Her astute best friend wasn't letting it go. And considering the fact Will's sister, and her best friend, Cleo, were both due for a girl's night, she needed the conversation over and done with. Fast.

She nodded. "I can't share. It's not my place. I'm just... worried." He'd seemed okay while he waited for her to finish her paper in the library. He was chatty enough during their lunch at the café, and he even asked her if she'd like to go out with him again. But she still couldn't shake the fact he wasn't okay.

Was she projecting? Was he really able to just be okay after opening that trunk of emotional trauma and releasing everything he'd let out?

"Happy Friday, fuckers!" Molly burst into their kitchen, bottle of Jack in one hand and a grease stained paper bag in the other. "I come bearing tacos."

Quinn couldn't help but laugh. Next to Molly, Cleo shook her head. "You'll have to excuse her. She doesn't get out much."

Bre snorted. "Sure, sure. Come in. You guys already know Quinn, right? She's leaving soon, she's got a…"

Quinn glared at her.

"Thing. She's got a thing."

Molly pointed the bottle at Quinn. "A date. With my brother, right?"

Quinn's eyes widened.

"Uh-huh. I talk to my mom regularly, missy. Okay, so the gossip tree is a few weeks behind." Molly pulled out a stool at the breakfast bar, grabbed a tortilla chip and slid it through the salsa before crunching it between her teeth. "So you and Willy, huh? How'd that happen?"

Molly picked up another chip, this time loading it with sour cream and guac. Her expression flattened. "How is he? We haven't spoken much since…" She shrugged. "Is he okay?"

It wasn't her story to tell, she needed to close ranks and respect his privacy. Even if she did think he would benefit from telling his family. It wasn't her decision to make.

"He's good."

"Where's he taking you, somewhere fun I hope? The boy needs to have more fun." Molly slugged JD straight from the bottle while Cleo tutted and pulled glasses from the cupboard behind Bre.

"It's a shame you can't stay and get drunk with us. I could pick your brain and make you tell me everything. He's not a very open person, so it's hard to get a read on him sometimes. But you…" Molly wagged a finger. "You seem like a much more open book."

She smiled. "I'd sing like a canary and tell you everything without even a drop. I'm a compulsive over-sharer."

"I like that." Molly took another pull from the bottle.

"He's taking me to the raceway."

Three sets of raised eyebrows met her from across the breakfast bar.

"Motorsports?" Quinn shrugged, her cheeks heating.

More silence.

"I like Formula One Racing – my cousin's a racecar driver for one of the teams over in Europe." Another shrug. "I told Will I liked motorsport and they're racing this weekend at Ogilvie. So we're going to watch some cars."

"That sounds oddly romantic for my brother. I approve."

Cleo nodded. "It's very sweet."

Quinn grinned. "I mean, it's not as fun as ice racing, but my need for speed hasn't been fed in a while so I'm excited."

Molly frowned. "Ice racing?"

Sabrina popped open a new bag of chips and poured some into a dish. "Right? Quinn took me last winter. It's near JJ's Bird's Nest in Garrison. Can you believe it? Ice racing! Something that can only happen in the land of 10,000 frozen lakes, right?"

Sabrina rolled the top of the bag down and fastened it with a clip.

Molly gestured for Quinn to keep talking, clearly she didn't have enough information on the ice racing thing.

"For six weeks every winter, Borden Lake turns into a frozen oasis for race car drivers. It's cold, it's fun, it's free to watch. It's something crazy and different. They have eight different classes of cars. There are those with studs in them, and those without. Trucks and side-by-sides have races too."

Molly took another sip of her drink. "Sounds savage. We're adding it to our bucket list, Cho-Cho. I wanna watch fast cars skating on ice."

Cleo shuddered. "Ay. No. There aren't enough coats in the world that would make me stand outside in Minnesota in winter and watch people risk their lives." Ever the sensible one.

Molly rolled her eyes before pointing at Quinn. "Double date!"

"So what are you watching tonight since there's no ice?"

Cleo had saved her from committing to a double date with her boyfriend's sister – she was the real MVP.

"Just regular racing. Truth be told I'll watch anything with an engine." She dropped her voice. "I prefer it to hockey."

Shrieks and yells of dissention made her laugh out loud.

"Don't tell Willy, he'll be pissed you don't love his sport."

Quinn shrugged. "He already knows. I have space in my heart for two sports." She jerked open her zipped sweater to display her *'My Heart Belongs to a Snow Pirate'* t-shirt. "See?"

The doorbell chimed and her cheeks heated.

"That can't be him already." Molly checked the time on her phone. "It's early." She pouted. "We started our little girls' night early so I could pick your brain and get to know you better."

Quinn started toward the door with a sympathetic smile. "Races start at 6.30PM, and it takes just over an hour to get there. But we can totally hang out another time, though."

"I'll hold you to that." Molly speared a finger at Cleo, then Sabrina. "You both heard that. She's gonna hang with me."

Quinn's stomach clenched. She'd need to make sure Will was on board with her spending time with his sister. Maybe she could convince Bre to come along and act like a buffer. The last thing she wanted was to put herself in the position of being in a room alone with the shrewd Morrison sibling.

Even if Quinn *didn't* know Will's secret, she still wouldn't have wanted to risk Molly fileting her like a steak.

Pulling the door open, she widened her eyes at Will. "Molly's here." Her whisper drew his brows up, but his wide smile didn't waver.

"You look great." He pulled her to him and kissed her cheek.

She smoothed her palms over the thighs of her jeans and tugged on the hem of her plaid shirt hanging loose over her tee. "Thanks, I feel like I should be going to a hootenanny rather than to watch racing, but I kinda love it."

His shoulders shook with silent laughter. "You don't need to defend your fashion choice to me, Q. We're gonna work on your ability to just accept a compliment."

"Q, now? We've dropped the rest of Quinny?"

"You're a Star Trek fan. It occurred to me that calling you Q would be kinda appropriate."

She laughed. "I don't hate it."

"If you're canoodling with my brother out there I'm gonna puke." Molly made gagging noises behind her.

"You wanna come in and say hey?"

Will shook his head but peered around the door, tossing a wave. "We're going to be late if we don't hit the road."

Molly snorted. "A likely excuse. This isn't over, Willy." She pointed a taco at Quinn. "We're hanging out. I'm getting your digits from Bre. It's happening." Was she putting on a brave face for Quinn? It sure as heck didn't seem as though things were as bad between Will and Molly as he'd said. But appearances could be deceiving.

She nodded as Will grabbed her hand and they left, closing the door behind them. "So, you wanna hang out with Molly, eh?" He raised his eyebrow as he opened his car door for her.

"*Want* is a strong word. They started their girls' night early so she could get to know me a bit better, and I'm hauling ass to go watch cars speed around a track. She wants to get to know me." She shrugged as she clipped her seatbelt in. "I don't blame her. As much as she intimidates me, I want to get to know her, too."

He circled the car and climbed into the driver's seat. "Molly intimidates you?"

She nodded. "She's so strong, and fierce... Her confidence is a thing dreams are made of. She's basically my hero." Saying it out loud made her feel utterly ridiculous, even more so because she'd said it to Molly's brother. She dropped her voice. "Every girl I know wants to be her. I know. I sound like a pathetic high school girl wanting in with the cool kids, right?"

Will shook his head, concentrating on the road as he weaved through traffic. "Not at all. It's important for women of all ages to have strong role models. Actually..." He frowned. "It's important for people of all ages to have strong role models. Everyone needs someone to look up to. We lucked out with Mom and Dad. Not everyone has that."

He smiled. "I'm pretty proud of her, even if I have a shitty way of showing it. I don't think she has any idea how much I envy her either. I'd love a fraction of her confidence and unwavering self-belief."

He threaded his hand into Quinn's as he spoke. "I mean, I know I'm considered attractive." A flush swept up his neck and made the tips of his ears red. "But she's unapologetically herself, y'know?"

Oh, she knew.

"She's known since she was little what she wanted to do with her life and pursued it relentlessly." He flicked his turn signal on and changed lanes. "I'm already out of college and I can't figure out what the hell I'm supposed to be doing with my life."

She squeezed his hand. "Not everyone can be the Molly Morrisons of the world. Give it time. It'll come."

CHAPTER 14
Quinn

B y the time they pulled up to Will's apartment she was exhausted. Their faces were both pink from sitting in the hot late afternoon sun, and Will's shirt was splattered with ketchup and mustard from the exploding hot dog that had left her doubled over with laughter.

He'd admitted to being surprised at how much fun watching racing could be, and he'd even said he'd love to go back again. Mission accomplished. She'd made him a fan. She'd awarded him bonus points for not fleeing or being outwardly judgmental at her cheering like a wild woman during the races.

Mercifully, he hadn't seen her at a hockey game.

"You sure you're okay?" She mumbled through a yawn as he led the way up to his apartment. He really seemed fine. But that was the problem. He was too fine, as though he hadn't a care in the world, which served only to make her even more concerned.

He couldn't possibly have gone from sobbing in her arms for hours on end to being okay. He'd admitted he was an over-achiever and had pushed himself even harder in school through his trauma as a teenager. Was he doing the same thing again? Burying it and plodding through?

"Will? You okay?"

"Yeah." He copied her yawn. "Just sleepy. It's late."

It was. And she didn't want to push too hard, but there was definitely something not right with him, she was sure of it. She had no proof, but her Spidey sense told her he was putting on a brave face which stung considering how close she'd felt to him the night he'd told her about his past. "I'll grab us some water."

He nodded. "I'm gonna go make sure my sheets are clean."

"I'm really too tired to care right now." She made her way into the kitchen, grabbed glasses and filled them from the dispenser in his fridge. A scrunched up granola bar wrapper lay at her feet and she put the glasses down to throw it in the trash. She flipped open the lid and paused, disbelief crashing into her at the sight of the leaflets she'd given him to read poking out of the top of the trashcan.

She huffed out a breath. Maybe he'd read them and tossed them when he'd finished. She picked them up and turned them over. They'd been ripped in half. Yeah. Something was definitely wrong with Will. Even if he wasn't ready to admit it.

It was unfair of her to feel in any way betrayed, but she did. He'd told her he'd read the material and talk to someone. He'd even shown her the numbers Austin had given him before she'd left his house the morning after his revelation.

She stormed toward the door, chest heaving, but stuttered to a halt with a sigh at the sight of a sleeping Will. His chest rose and fell with heavy, even breaths. He looked so peaceful. She needed to make space for him, to let him process, and to come to terms with everything in his own time.

She put the leaflets back in the trash and made her way back to the bedroom where her phone was vibrating. She put

the glasses on the nightstand and grabbed a shirt to sleep in
from Will's drawer before checking her messages.

> Nova: Hey babe, it's Nova. I was wondering
> if you had given any thought to baking for
> some of the moms on the team.

Perhaps texting Nova would distract her from wanting to
wake Will up and demand to know what the hell was going on
with him. As worried as she was about him, she needed to cool
down.

> Nova: Namely: me. I'm 'some of the moms.'

> Nova: It's Huck's birthday next week and he
> needs the best cake in town.

> Nova: Pleeeeease? ::Pleading eye emoji::

She couldn't help but laugh. The woman was persistent.

> Quinn: You know it's the middle of the
> night, right?

> Nova: The same thing could be said to you.
> At least I have a good excuse. The middle
> of the night is the only time I don't have
> three kids following me around saying my
> name eleventy billion times.

> Nova: It's the only time of the day I can
> poop without two dozen fingers clawing at
> the edges of the door to get in like
> something out of a horror movie.

> Nova: It's the only time I can eat a candy
> bar without having to hide inside the closet
> for a blissful two minutes to shove it in my
> face.

> Nova: What's your excuse? Why are you up
> so late?

Nova: OMG are you getting hot sexy times with Coach Mo?

Nova: PUH-LEASE tell me you're getting hot sexy times with Coach Mo!! ::eyeball emoji::

She covered her face to smother her giggles and slipped into the bathroom to take off her makeup and pee before bed. She snapped a screenshot of herself on the edge of Will's tub.

Quinn: No sexy times here.

Nova: Ugh. How can I live vicariously through you if you're not doing the dirty with the hunky Coach?

Quinn: We *did* go out on a date tonight though. That's all I'm giving you.

Nova: For now. I'm gleefully rubbing my hands together. I want an invite to the wedding.

Nova: Right. Enough cock-chat, it's time for cake-chat. Please?

Nova: It's just three dozen cupcakes. You could do that in your sleep.

Nova was right, she could.

Quinn: I'm not saying yes… but for the sake of discussion, what flavor(s) did you have in mind.

Nova: Yes! I knew you'd say yes.

Quinn rolled her eyes but couldn't stop from grinning. Nova was certainly determined.

Nova: I don't want to hinder your creative
deliciousness. Know what? Make it easy.
An even four dozen cupcakes, two flavors,
dealer's choice.

She both loved and hated when people gave her free rein to make whatever she wanted, especially when she didn't even know Nova or Huck all that well. Her stomach thrashed and her heart raced. It was what she'd always wanted, people to want her delicious treats.

WWMMD?

What would Molly Morrison do?

That badass would say 'Hell-fucking-yes, sign me up!'

Gnawing on her lip, she typed with trembling fingers.

Quinn: What's the theme of the party?

Nova: He's obsessed with Mario Kart.

Quinn: Hmm. Okay, what about orange
creamsicle, and chocolate honeycomb?

Nova: I'm drooling on my phone.

She smiled again. The woman certainly knew how to flatter.

Quinn: Fine. I'll do it. But just for you.

Nova: About that...

She shook her head. No. One kid's birthday party was enough to get her feet wet, to test the waters, to see what it would be like to work for someone other than herself.

> Nova: Tristan's mom is here too. We had a
> mom sleepover (translation: she drank too
> much wine and couldn't drive home.)
> Tristan's birthday party is the day after
> Huck's. You wouldn't make her resort to
> store bought cupcakes now, would you?
> ::Pleading eye emoji:: ::Pleading eye emoji::

Her stomach tightened. It was already spiraling out of her control. And once the other moms in the hockey team heard she'd made cupcakes for two parties, they'd push her to make them, too.

She walked back into the bedroom, and eased herself onto the bed next to Will. He believed in her. He believed in her so much, he'd even written a proposal to help make her dreams come true. Was it time to start daring to believe in herself?

WWMMD?

She'd dive in with both feet.

> Nova: Or worse… GASP. Please tell me
> you're not going to make me share MY
> cupcakes. ::cringe emoji::
>
> Nova: Nova doesn't share food.

Nova sent a GIF of Joey from *Friends* that said 'Joey doesn't share food.' Quinn smothered a snort.

She'd make cupcakes for Huck and Tristan's parties. She'd make sure it didn't interfere with her studies or her duties at the shelter. She'd dip her toe into the idea of being a responsible, capable business woman and hope she didn't drown.

❄

Falling asleep in Will's arms had been nigh on impossible. She'd tossed and turned all night, anxiety raking up her spine and fixing her in a choke hold. No sooner had she sent a reply to Nova saying she'd do both parties, than her inner loud mouth, the voice of dissension and self-criticism reminded her that she was *not* in fact, Molly Morrison.

When she'd finally given up and made her way to the kitchen to brew coffee, the ripped up flyers still taunted her from the trash.

Seeing them the night before, she'd felt judgment. How could he not have followed through on the information she'd collated for him? How could he not want to talk to someone? To make things better? To pursue justice for himself after all those years of suffering?

That wasn't fair, and she didn't mean to judge. Everyone was different and some take a long time to process their abuse while others bury it for their entire lives. She was determined to help Will so he didn't end up being one of those people

Staring at the garbage while cooking breakfast, she saw everything in a new light. She'd clearly upset him enough to tear up the resources. They weren't just tossed away, they were destroyed. Her stomach clenched.

Despite her desire for justice, for Will and the other victims, she'd probably pressed a little too hard considering how long he'd buried everything. Had she accidentally hurt him even more?

"Hey." Will's sleep-filled voice made her jump.

"Morning." She yawned. "Coffee is in the pot and I was making breakfast burritos but they're more like breakfast tacos right now, you only have tiny tortillas. Weirdo."

"Sounds good to me." His warm hand met her lower back and she closed her eyes for a moment, absorbing his calm.

"You didn't sleep well. Was being in my bed all that scary for you?" He kissed her cheek, reaching over her head to grab a mug from the cupboard.

"Not at all. I kinda loved it. I borrowed a shirt to sleep in, and I'll probably need to borrow another one to get home if that's okay?"

"Of course. Wanna talk about what kept you up all night?"

She snuck a sidelong glance at him and damn near choked on her own spit. While messy bed hair made her look like a freakin' disheveled yeti, it worked for Will. He looked like he had stepped straight out of the glossy pages of an underwear catalog.

Barefoot, shirtless, boxer briefs riding low on his hips, and that perfect, perky bubble butt calling for her to sink her teeth into. Fuck.

An acrid smell met her nose. She was going to burn breakfast and set the house on fire if she didn't pay attention to what she was doing.

As she shuffled food around in the pan, his hand met her hip and he spoke close to her ear. "Try not to set off the fire alarm; it's still early. I don't want to piss off the neighbors; I kinda like them."

Her face was as hot as the pan she was using. Rolling her lips between her teeth, she nodded, giving him an "m-hmm" as an answer.

He pulled out a chair and sat, but from the warmth radiating through the back of her shirt, he hadn't stopped staring at her.

"Nova messaged me last night."

He cleared his throat. "Oh?"

"Yeah. She didn't say where she got my number from."

"Is that so?" His fake nonchalance wasn't fooling her. She knew *precisely* how Nova had snagged her number.

"Uh huh. She gave me hers at the arena, but I didn't give her mine back. Odd, huh? Anyway, she wants me to make cupcakes for Huck's party."

"That's cool." While his voice was largely calm, it was also tinged with excitement. "Are you going to do it?"

She nodded, scooping scrambled eggs onto the plate that had been kept warm in the oven. She put two plates on the table between them. Warm tortillas, bacon, potato cubes with melted cheese, scrambled eggs, and mixed bell peppers and onions. Did a more perfect breakfast exist?

I think not.

"Bacon makes everything better." He was already folding a slice into his mouth, sexy sounds that made her want to abandon the food and offer herself as breakfast instead rumbling in his throat.

Down girl.

Will was already halfway through his first taco with only one bite. Filling spilled out the end and onto his plate.

"She wants four dozen cupcakes."

"Is she inviting every kid in Minnesota?"

She laughed. "I guess so. She has three of her own, plus the hockey team." She whistled. "That's a lot of kids."

"They're a great bunch. Makes it easy to see myself with a big family in the future."

She sucked in a breath and a chunk of potato. Her eyes watered, as she grabbed her glass of orange juice and chugged it, praying for it to dislodge both the food and the panic stuck in the back of her throat.

His smile turned to a frown. "Don't want kids?" He got a jar of salsa and a spoon.

Damn he wasn't fucking around with the tough questions, was he? Something must have registered on her face because his cheeks turned pink.

"I'm not saying right away. But some day. I'm too young

to be a father." He chuckled but stopped dead. "Though seeing Russ with Jude... I dunno. It doesn't make me want to have one right this second, but it comforts me in the fact that if it had happened by now, I probably could have handled it just fine."

Ouch. Shots fired.

Her taco turned to acid in her stomach. She'd never doubted her decision to terminate her pregnancy.

And her better judgment knew he wasn't assessing her – he couldn't, he didn't know her story. But the shame and guilt society had conditioned her to feel about her right to choose was being stabbed into her chest by every word that came from his mouth.

It wasn't that she didn't want kids; it was that she felt as though she didn't deserve them. After having her abortion a couple of years ago, she was constantly at war with herself. It had been the right thing to do at the time. It had. She was under no illusions. She hadn't been in a position to offer a life to a kid.

But she couldn't help but wonder if she'd ever feel ready for a child, and if she did, would she deserve to be a mother when she'd terminated a pregnancy?

She opened her mouth to answer Will's question, unsure of what would come out, when his phone rang. She ate in silence as he talked to Erika, her thoughts too loud for her to even pick up what they were talking about.

He rolled his eyes and mouthed "sorry" as his mom kept chatting. She finished her taco, put her dishes in the dishwasher, and hooked a thumb over her shoulder toward the door to indicate she was going to get changed.

He nodded, holding two fingers up. She dressed in Will's clothes with a heavy heart, not just about her previous choices, but her future, too, wholly overwhelmed by the prospect of stepping forward into her dreams. Fear of failure, fear of success, impostor syndrome... they all prodded at her with pointy sticks.

"Sorry about that." Will joined her in the bedroom. "Mom says she only wants to chat for a second and suddenly we're down the rabbit hole talking about something she saw on TV, and I can't escape." He rubbed at the back of his neck, and she managed a small smile.

"Why the sad face, Q?"

"I'm okay. Just..." She spread her hands. "Overwhelmed. I'm going to go home and work on some assignments to free up some time to make these cupcakes for the hockey moms next week."

He kissed her forehead. "You want to grab dinner tomorrow?"

She couldn't meet his eyes. She needed to get her shit together. Either he was sad too and doing a really good job of covering it up, or he really was fine and if that was the case, she didn't need to taint him with her sadness.

Forcing positivity into her voice, she smiled. "Rain check? I really gotta get some work done this weekend."

Uncertainty flickered across his face, but he didn't press her. It was one of the things she both loved and hated about him in equal measure.

"Sure thing." He pulled her to him, his warmth engulfing her and slipped his hands around her face before kissing her deeply.

Describing a kiss was always difficult, it was the same thing every time, right? Two mouths pressed against each other, lips moving, and tongues colliding. But the tenderness with which he kissed her brought tears to her eyes and left her breathless and yearning for more.

She nibbled and sucked on his lips, losing herself in his touch, his taste, his hunger for her. When they pulled back for breath, his eyes were almost golden in the morning light streaming through his blinds.

Maybe if she kept kissing him, real life would be kept at bay. Maybe she wouldn't have to see if her idea for a business would sink or swim, and maybe she could somehow convince Will that keeping everything inside wasn't a good idea for anyone.

Especially him.

CHAPTER 15

Will

Quinn's gloomy face as he pulled away from the curb outside her apartment had stuck with him all day. Was she upset that he'd given her number to Nova? Was she upset that she didn't want kids and he did? Churning through potential causes for her downturned lips and dull eyes wasn't helping his mood.

Neither was the score of the hockey game unfolding on the ice. He'd stepped in to coach for the First Mates at the last minute. Their stand-in coach had left them in the lurch, and he'd agreed to jump in so they didn't have to forfeit.

3-0 down in the middle of the second, and he wished he hadn't volunteered at all. Rationally speaking, he knew their losing had almost nothing to do with his coaching. They were a new-to-him team, and he was a new coach to them.

He couldn't blame them for being disjointed in their plays when the uncertainty of their team hung over them every time they took to the ice. And by all accounts, every coach they'd had before taught them something different.

But to him, it was simply one more thing he sucked at. The kids had promise, raw talent, and if someone would just stick around long enough to coach them properly, he was convinced they could go all the way. He hoped that Austin's dad would come through for the players and they'd be able to find someone truly great to lead the team.

There was no doubt in his mind he was watching future Snow Pirates, then NHL-ers skating in front of him, but he just couldn't find a way to get through to them.

When the whistle blew to call an end to the second period, they were down by five. His chest ached. As he turned to make his way down the tunnel, he caught a glimpse of Quinn sitting in the stands.

She had an oversized Snow Pirates hoodie on that came to her knees as she sat and a green bobble hat with earflaps and wool braids that hung down over her shoulders. She tossed him a shy wave, pulling her lip between her teeth. The wrinkles in her forehead and across the bridge of her nose were adorable.

She was clearly worried about him.

In truth, he was kind of worried about himself, too. He'd *almost* made an appointment with one of the therapists Austin had recommended, but he'd stopped himself.

He'd almost told his parents, but he'd stopped himself.

He'd almost called Finn to catch up, but he'd stopped himself.

Emotion pooled in his stomach, sizzling and burning. While he wanted to do something about Ms. Phillips, he was also scared. Of what, he wasn't entirely sure.

Maybe he was scared they'd judge him for keeping quiet for so long, enabling Phillips to potentially hurt other kids. Maybe he was scared she'd point the finger at him and say he was the one who assaulted her. Maybe he was afraid they'd look at him with sympathetic eyes, or they'd feel guilty that they didn't know and couldn't help him at the time.

Maybe it was a combination of everything.

He swallowed, waved back at her, and followed the team down the tunnel to the changing room.

Whatever it was that stopped him from sharing, that made him tear up the flyers Quinn had given to him, that gave him pause every time he picked up the phone to call the number Austin had given him, it was unrelenting.

He felt like he was stuck in cement, unable to turn around and take back the words he'd shared with Quinn, and unable to move forward. Pressure squeezed the breath from his body, making it hard to think, to speak, to act.

Ironically, if one of his friends, or someone on the team he was coaching came to him and said they were being abused, he'd help. He'd advocate for them until his voice went hoarse and he'd done every damn thing he could for them. But he felt like he should have done more, he should somehow be stronger, like he needed to keep it all inside, and make sure no one else hurt like he did.

Raking his hand through his hair, he hissed out a long, slow breath. His head pounded behind his eyes, and his muscles ached with a tiredness he couldn't seem to shift no matter how much sleep he got.

The game ended 8-1. At least the visiting team hadn't bagged a shutout.

It was a small consolation for the crestfallen kids in his locker room as they changed back into their civvies, but it was something. Their melancholy was a living breathing creature that expanded to fill every inch of space between the kids as they changed in silence.

Dejected eyes met his as each of the kids left the locker room to go home. The youngest of the team, a recent transfer from out of town, approached him as the rest of the team trudged to the exit.

"Are you our coach now?"

The little hope-filled voice shattered his heart. He

crouched so he was at the kid's level. "Not full time, lil dude. But we're working on securing funding for the team. New equipment, new uniforms, new coaching staff... we're trying our hardest to give you guys the best."

The little boy dropped his stick and threw his arms around Will's shoulders. "You're the best coach." He grabbed his stick and hurried out the door.

Will pushed out a whoosh of air and stood, scrubbing his palms over his face. When he removed his hands, Quinn stood in front of him with tears in her eyes.

"That was the single most adorable thing I've ever seen."

He nodded, but couldn't answer, afraid that if he opened his mouth, he'd cry, too.

She launched herself at him, almost strangling him with her arms around his neck. "You're doing something great with these kids, you know?"

It was nice of her to say, but he didn't feel like he was doing anywhere near what he should be.

It wasn't enough. And no matter how many kids he helped going forward, his mind would always tug him back to those who probably got hurt because of his silence.

The cracks in his heart spread.

"You ready to leave or do you have stuff to do? Wanna walk out together?"

He nodded and followed her outside. "Thanks for coming this afternoon. You really didn't have to. I appreciate the support though. Truly."

She smiled and turned to get into her car. "No sweat. You know I'd never miss an excuse to scream at referees. Even if I have to filter out my cussing for sensitive little ears."

"Hold up!" Nova ran toward them from a car she abandoned at the edge of the parking lot, waving a piece of paper in her hand.

She presented them both with a flier. Actually, the bright

colored superheroes and 'You are Invited' across the top of the leaflet suggested it wasn't a flier, it was a party invitation.

"Huck wants you both at his party next weekend." She reached into her back pocket and produced a second invitation that she handed to him. "Tristan wants you at his, too. And his mom, Arden, said you can bring a plus one." She gave a not-too-subtle head jerk toward Quinn who giggled.

"You really don't have to do this." Quinn waved the invite. "It's very sweet, but you don't—"

Nova narrowed her eyes. "Listen here, Quinnifred – I watched Hocus Pocus last night and decided you're a hotter version of Winnifred, but you have every ounce of her sass and then some. So I've decided that's your new nickname now. Anyways, my son will be utterly heartbroken if you don't attend his party."

Wow. Her acting game was strong. She had the fake sad face and the dramatic distress in her voice. Quinn wasn't buying it any more than he was, but they both let Nova continue.

"Okay, fine. His mom will be heartbroken if you don't attend. Whatever. I feel like you need some adulty guidance right now, and I've nominated myself as that adult. Come along, watch people reacting to your crack-cakes and then tell me you don't want to make people smile like that every day."

There it was. Her motivation was pure and delightful. Will couldn't have agreed more with her reason for inviting Q, but he didn't want to react in case it spooked her.

"Huck *really* wants *you* to go, Coach." She fluttered her eyelashes at him as though it would make a difference to his answer. "You can't break the kid's little heart, can you?"

Quinn's raised eyebrows, expectant stare, and lips tucked between her teeth as she failed to fight a smile made him laugh. "No. I can't break Huck's little heart. I'll be there." He folded his arms and quirked his brows at Quinn. Her turn.

She studied the invitation in her hands for a long moment before lifting her head. Both Nova and Will stared at her, then each other, then back to Quinn.

"There'll be alcohol..." Nova sing-songed. "Oh come on! It'll be fun."

Quinn sighed and shook her head, the hand with the flier dropped to her side like she was admitting defeat. "Fine." A shrug. "Why the hell not?"

"Atta girl! I mean, I coulda done with a little more excitement but I'll take it." Nova gave her a gentle shove on the shoulder. "Trust me. You'll look back on this moment in a few years and you'll thank me." She winked. "I'll take my thanks in cupcakes. I'm not fussy on the flavor. I'm a total Quinn-Cake slut. Right." She clapped her hands together. "I guess we'll see you both next weekend then."

Wondering what the hell he'd really signed up for, he nodded. "I guess you will."

While they hadn't seen each other for the entire week between the First Mates' game and Huck's party, they'd texted back and forth a little. He'd been grateful for the space she'd given him to process his feelings on everything that had happened.

Or he would have been had he actually taken time to process them. Instead, he'd done manual labor every day with his dad at his parents' house. They'd decided to tear out their old kitchen and put in a new one, and it kind of sounded like a fun distraction and a way to clear his mind.

But Quinn had declined a ride to the party, and she'd been short with him, too short. He was starting to think she might not have given him a week of space, but rather he'd made the assumption that's what it was, and taken it.

Sitting in his car around the corner from Nova's house, he swallowed.

He still hadn't called to talk to anyone about his assault. He still hadn't told his family. Nothing had changed.

Quinn had been so amped up about bringing justice down on Ms. Phillip's head that she'd probably be upset to know he hadn't done a damned thing since they'd last talked. He tried to shake off the guilt gnawing at his insides.

Rationally speaking, he just wasn't ready. And in everything he'd read about sexual assault victims on the internet, they had to be ready to talk about their experiences.

He sighed. She'd just have to sit with her disappointment until he found his voice.

He made his way to Nova's front door, not expecting Quinn would be the one to open it dressed like Daisy from Super Mario. Then again, he shouldn't have been surprised. Quinn wasn't one to half-ass anything. She did everything whole-assed and as a gamer, he appreciated her efforts.

She pulled the door wide, standing in her yellow and burnt orange dress that poofed out at the waist. She wore a golden crown tucked into her red mane and a nervous smile on her face.

"Hey." She stepped back too far for him to kiss her cheek as he walked into the house and when she closed the door behind him, she still kept her distance.

He winced. Yeah. She was upset at him. Whether it was for not doing anything with the pamphlets she'd given him, or for not seeing her for an entire week, he wasn't sure.

But a kid's birthday party was hardly the place to talk about such things. He crammed his hands into the front pockets of his jeans and rocked on his heels. "I love the costume. Was I supposed to wear a costume? I didn't see it mentioned anywhere on the invite."

"I'm surprised you read it." She didn't say it at full volume, but it was loud enough. Her eyes flexed wide and she slipped her thumbnail between her teeth, shaking her head. "I just figured…" She shrugged. "It's a kid's party, and I already had the costume from Halloween a few years ago. Nova nearly lost her mind when she saw it. And Huck is so excited to have Daisy at his party."

"You look great."

She did. He was having incredibly confusing and naughty thoughts about bending 'Daisy' over the back of Nova's black leather couch and fucking her senseless while standing among kid's birthday party decorations and balloons. Without the kids present, of course.

"Coach Mo!" Nova spread her arms wide and grabbed him in a hug. "So good of you to come." She stepped back, a smug grin on her face. "Doesn't Quinn look darling as Daisy? Huck was super thrilled." She grabbed his elbow, making the gift bag in his hand swing. "Come and see her cupcakes. They. Are. Ah-Ma-Zing."

Quinn's face was almost the color of her hair as the three of them made their way into the party room. He dropped his present onto the gift table as they passed and weaved his way through the parents milling around the drinks station to get to the desserts.

"You can totally take one." Nova elbowed him with a wink. "I won't tell anyone."

Sitting at the top of the cupcake pyramid sat a small cake, with a fondant scene from Mario Kart decorating it. Beneath the centerpiece were two flavors of cupcakes alternating around the cake stand. On top of each cupcake was a fondant recreation of the characters' faces from the game.

They must have taken her forever to make, and they looked too good to eat.

"Try one." Nova insisted.

Glancing at Quinn for assurance that she wasn't going to kill him for demolishing one of her masterpieces, he picked up a cupcake from the side labeled orange creamsicle, peeled back the wrapper, and took an embarrassingly large bite.

He closed his eyes to savor the mouthful. The frosting was perfectly sweet. The cake was light, airy and so fresh it almost dissolved in his mouth. The orange flavor was detectable but not overpowering. Fuck she was good.

"I know, right? I made noises like that too, but they weren't nearly as hot as all that."

When he opened his eyes, Nova was fanning herself and Q's face had somehow gone even redder.

He licked his lips, determined not to waste a single crumb of the delicious miniature piece of art he wanted to stuff in his face. "This is so freakin' good, Q."

The small smile teasing the edges of her mouth burst into a wide grin. "Yeah?" She heaved the word out on a sigh, like she'd been holding her breath for hours waiting for his opinion.

He nodded. "Raspberry and lemon are still my favorite though. And your apple pie is only second to my own mom's, but this..." He raised the cupcake in his hand before taking another large bite. "Mmmmm. So good." He didn't even care that he was speaking with his mouth full. The look of sheer pride on Quinn's face was worth it.

Someone called Quinn to a group of kids waiting to have their picture taken. Taking in the party he realized that he'd never seen such an extravagant kid's party. From the popcorn and cotton candy machines and face painter to the bounce house in the backyard, Nova had spared no expense for Huck. He made small talk with the parents of his hockey kids, ate more than his fair share of cupcakes, and kept a roaming eye on Quinn as she worked the room.

Most of the kids wanted their photo taken with her in her get-up, so she was kept busy, but he couldn't help feeling like she was keeping her distance.

When he finally found her hiding behind the chocolate fountain – or rather, attempting to hide because there was no hiding such a loud and frilly dress, the party was winding down. He walked up beside her and grabbed a marshmallow and a skewer.

"I feel like I might have misread the situation this week, and I'm sorry." It was better to own his mistake off the bat than to let it fester anymore. He didn't want to bicker about it. "I figured you were giving me space to process things, so I took it. It didn't occur to me that you might be waiting for me to call, or... I dunno, something."

She pulled the giant strawberry from the falling waves of chocolate, cradling a paper plate underneath to catch the drips. "Or something."

Her green eyes darkened.

At the front door, Nova waved goodbye to a few of the parents. Huck and one of his friends were on the bounce house out in the yard, and despite it only being the two of them in such a big room, the air felt thin.

Cramming the marshmallow into his mouth, he searched the cupboards under the sink for the trash bags... When he finally straightened, brandishing his prize, Quinn held out her hand for one.

As they tidied, the unpleasant silence between them swelled, suffocating. He had to fill it, he needed to say something. "I didn't call anyone to talk about... it... not yet."

"You don't say." Her passive aggressive skills were on point.

He bristled. Screw her. He was the victim. "I'm just not ready, Quinn."

She slapped the trash bag against her thigh. "Then you *say* that to me, William." She huffed and shook her head.

Fighting while cleaning up a kid's birthday party hadn't been on his agenda, and they weren't alone, not really.

"You don't take the resources I put together for you... to *help* you. Then tear them up and throw them away like garbage."

His stomach dropped. She'd found the leaflets in the trash. She knew not only that he hadn't called anyone, but that he wasn't planning to use any of the information she'd assembled for him since he'd thrown it all away.

Fuck. He rubbed the back of his neck, the soft hair at his nape providing little comfort from the prickly redhead in front of him.

"Maybe if you hadn't been so full on, I wouldn't have reacted the way I did."

"Maybe if I'd..." She murmured his words back to herself. Her eyes widened and her shoulders sagged.

He balled his hands into fists by his sides. "Yeah. And maybe if you weren't so fucking self-righteous—"

A small gasp escaped her.

"And judgmental—"

She gasped again like he'd struck her, but he was already finishing his sentence. "—you'd have noticed that I wasn't ready to talk, or to take it further." He pointed at her. "You should know better from working at the shelter."

Her jaw hung open. Fury boiled in her eyes. She was pissed.

Good. So was he. He was pissed at his teacher for violating him. He was pissed at her other victims for gloating about it and making him feel like he couldn't speak up for himself.

At his parents for not noticing anything was wrong, even though he'd worked so hard to hide it.

At Finn for being with his sister and abandoning him.

At Quinn for being so easy to talk to that it had all broken free from the lockbox he'd tucked inside his chest.

But most of all, he was pissed at himself, for letting it happen, for becoming a victim, for not speaking out right away, for keeping it buried for so long... the list was endless.

Wait. What had she just said? No, surely not... He turned to her smoldering, scowling face.

"Wh-what?"

"I said." She swallowed and patted down the top layer of yellow tulle on her dress. "I'm done."

"B-because I didn't call someone?"

"Because if you think I'm being self-righteous and judgmental..." She used her fingers as quotation marks. "Then you don't know me at all."

Nova stepped into the room. "Man, did it get cold in here?" She folded her arms and rubbed her biceps. She chuckled, but her clear attempt at humor fell flat.

"I have to go." Quinn's pained eyes never left his.

"Oh. No problem." Nova approached the counter. "Let me just grab my purse so I can pay you."

But Quinn was already walking, no, running out the door. He turned to follow her but Nova stopped him with a hand on his arm. "I feel like she might need some space right now."

"You heard?"

Nova nodded.

He sighed. Apparently calling his girlfriend self-righteous and judgmental had been the kiss of death for their relationship.

But she had been both those things.

He finished picking up the trash and cleaning up in silence

with Nova before leaving. Sitting in his car, staring at the steering wheel, he had no idea what to do or where to go.

Before the incident with Molly and Finn he'd have been able to call Finn and talk things through with him, but everything was different. He couldn't.

He could try Austin but for as close as they were, the idea of maybe crying in front of his strong and stoic friend just made him even more determined *not* to call him.

So he set off for home. If anyone could fix the mess he'd wound up in, it would be Mom and Dad.

He hoped.

CHAPTER 16

Quinn

"Fuck him. I did nothing wrong." She punched her pillow. "Right?" She nodded and punched it again. "Right." Fortunately for both her and the pillow, it didn't have an opposing opinion. "I was there for him. I was supportive, helpful, I pulled together pamphlets for him. I gave him everything he needed to take the next steps."

A growl rattled through her chest. Self-righteous. Self-fucking-righteous. Was he for real?

Self-righteous.

She grunted, then fell face-first onto the bed and screamed, thrashing her hands and feet against the soft fabric of her quilt.

"I did nothing wrong." She repeated her words but with less gusto. She had done nothing wrong.

Right?

Or had she? Was this on her?

She rolled onto her back and ran through the past few weeks in her mind as she stared at the ceiling. She should have kept her mouth closed at the party. That much was clear. She should have taken a beat, calmed the fuck down, and held her tongue.

It had been her undoing. The combination of feeling queasy the whole time over the fact that people were eating her product and discussing it in front of her, and Will being so damn close while she silently fumed at him had sent her into a tailspin.

Her inner critic wouldn't STFU and leave her alone. She felt guilty for doing something fun, making something pretty and delicious for Huck and Tristan's parties rather than helping out at the shelter or studying. Or even figuring out a better way to help Will.

Her stomach sank.

She had failed him.

Both Nova and Tristan's mom had been happy with their baked goody deliveries. But considering she was standing in front of them, they couldn't really have said anything else, could they?

It's not like Nova had the time to say, 'Oh hey, I actually hate these and they don't taste the way I expected them to. Could you do them over, please?' considering she'd delivered them with sixty minutes to go until the party started.

Would she have still liked them if she'd seen them a week before the party? Would she have gone elsewhere?

Quinn's phone vibrated under her back and she writhed and groped until she found the damn thing.

Unknown Number: Hey Quinn, it is Austin. I
got your number from the paperwork Will
gave me. My father has given his blessing
for us to go ahead with your start-up
business loan. I have a whole bunch of
papers for you to look over and sign. I am
guessing you do not have an accountant
yet so I will bring one of the financial team
along to explain things to you. Just say
when and where.

She tossed her phone off the edge of the bed and burst out crying. Will had done it, he'd made her dreams come true. Sure, he'd used his connections to a wealthy friend to make it happen, but that was neither here nor there. He'd done it all the same.

He'd only gone and fucking done it.

And she was a shitty human being for making a victim of sexual assault feel like shit about himself.

She pulled the duvet over her head, and after a long and cathartic cry, she scooted to the edge of the bed and stretched to grab her phone before texting Pippa.

Quinn: SOS. Need advice.

Pippa: I'm at the shelter till 4pm. Bring
snacks.

She dragged herself out of bed with a huff before trudging to the kitchen and pulled baking supplies out onto the counter. A gut wrenching break up called for one thing and one thing only: Emergency apple pie.

By the time Sabrina got back after lunch with Russ and Jude, six apple pies sat cooling on racks in the kitchen, the place was spotless, and Quinn was watching *A Walk to Remember*. A classic romance movie that somehow managed to make her cry every freakin' time.

"Wanna talk about the explosion of apple pies in the kitchen?"

Quinn paused the heaped fork on its way to her mouth as Sabrina appeared in front of her, blocking her view of the TV.

"Nope." She popped the P. "Hard pass."

"Must be bad if you're halfway through an entire apple pie and watching movies that make you cry." Bre crouched in front of her. "Is it—?"

She waved her fork. "Don't say his name." Her chin trembled, hot tears burned at the back of her eyes.

"Oh, Quinny."

Shaking her head she whispered, "Don't." She couldn't even meet Sabrina's gaze. She knew the sadness and pity that were waiting for her.

Bre nodded and squeezed her hand. "Want me to stay? I won't come between you and that pie, but I can sit with you if you'd like."

"Nooooo. You have plans with Russ and Jude. I'm going to visit with Pippa soon. It's all good."

Bre pursed her lips and swiveled them from left to right. After a hefty pause, she nodded once. "I have my phone. If you need me, you'd better text." She looped her arms around Quinn and gave a tight squeeze. "Love you."

"Love you most."

From somewhere behind, Jude yelled, "Wuv you three thousand!"

Quinn's heart pinched. What a doll.

Two hours later Quinn had eaten an entire apple pie, showered, changed, and made her way to the shelter with a pie-in-hand.

She tapped on Pippa's office door. "I come bearing snacks."

Pippa gave a low whistle. "You baked your famous pie for

me. It must be serious. Come in. Sit." She jerked her chin at the seat across the table from her. "I'll take this."

She took the pie, unwrapped it, and dug a fork out of the top drawer of her desk before spearing into the dessert. "Don't judge me," she mumbled around a mouthful of flaky pastry. "I skipped lunch." She gestured at Quinn with a forkful of pie. "Spill."

Quinn sat on her hands, tugged them out, folded them in her lap, twisted them together, and then pulled at the hem of her *She-Ra* t-shirt.

Pippa dropped her fork, stood, leaned over the table and grabbed both her hands. "Quinn, stop. What is it?"

"Complete confidence?" Her jaw trembled and her mouth was dry.

"Of course."

"I have a male friend who has recently admitted to me that he was sexually assaulted by his teacher in high school a number of years ago. I put together a selection of leaflets from out front. I got him numbers and therapists' information... everything he'd need." She shook her head, still not completely sure what she'd done wrong.

"He..." She cleared her throat. "He didn't react well to it at all. I mean, I thought he did, he seemed fine. But later I found out that he tore up the leaflets and threw them away. He stalled on talking to a professional about it. He pulled back and even became..." She searched for a word. "Disconnected, I guess. It went the complete opposite direction to how I'd expected it to."

Pippa heaped a forkful of pie into her mouth and chewed, gesturing for Quinn to continue.

"I know I'm not a counselor, but I did the basic training when I first came to the shelter. I followed everything it said. I gave him space to talk about what he'd gone through, I gave him resources to follow through with... I thought I was doing the right thing."

Pippa sighed and tucked another bite into her mouth. "First of all, this is orgasmic, and I'm gonna need a regular hook up so it better be on the menu in your bakery. Secondly, if you'd gone into the face-to-face side of volunteering here, dealing with victims, you'd have done further training. But since you chose to do the fundraising stuff, it wasn't necessary since you rarely spend time with the people who use our services."

She didn't let Pippa finish before she barged ahead. "I just don't understand why he doesn't want the woman punished. Why doesn't he want justice for himself?"

Her friend's eyes softened. "The victims have to be ready to speak about what happened to them, Quinn. There are any number of reasons why someone wouldn't want to talk about what happened to them."

The older woman sighed. "Fear. Self-doubt. Lack of faith in the justice system to adequately punish the perpetrator of the assault." She held up her fingers counting them off as she spoke. "Those are the big ones, the overarching ones: a lot falls under those three. I imagine your friend is currently caught up in a lot of trauma that hasn't been addressed. But you can't force help on him, Quinn. He needs to be ready."

"And if he's not?" She bit her lip so hard she was surprised she couldn't taste blood.

"Like I said, you can't force him."

"What if he's never ready?"

Pippa's silent, miserable face was all the answer she needed.

Fuck. She'd fucked up.

She'd pushed Will so hard he'd stepped back from her and now they were broken. She'd managed to fuck up the best relationship she'd ever had when all she was trying to do was help.

S hake. "Quinny?" Another shake. Sabrina's weight settled on the bed next to her as she pulled the pillow away from Quinn's head. "Quinn, come on. Please. I'm starting to get really worried about you. It's been a week."

Quinn snorted. "It's been a couple days." She spoke into the mattress so it came out as a garbled mess.

"It's been a week. It's time to get up. I know you're sad, but I can't let you throw your future down the drain over a boy."

"I'm a terrible person."

"You're not."

She rolled onto her back, spitting hair out of her mouth as she did. "You don't know that."

"I've known you for long enough to know you're not. I need you to get up, get a shower, eat something that doesn't come wrapped in plastic, and get your shit together." Sabrina brushed more hair back from her face.

"Whatever is going on with you can't be fought from your hovel of filth. I lied to your professors. I told them all you're sick, and I grabbed notes from people in your class and copied them for you. Pippa said if you're not back at the shelter tomorrow she's coming over herself. And Russell says you haven't replied to Austin yet about the startup loan. Girl. Don't make me slap you. I refuse to let you self-sabotage this."

Bre sucked in a huge breath when she got to the end of her speech. "I don't know what happened, and if you still don't want to talk about it, that's okay, but we gotta get you vertical and functioning. And I won't take no for an answer."

Sabrina's stern face needed some work, it was still soft and adorable, but the concern swirling in her friend's eyes was enough to make her sit up.

"It's been a week?"

Bre nodded. "I get that you want some time to yourself, but you can't isolate from the world like this. It's not healthy."

She'd gone from an emotional, reactive mess to numb in a week. And were it not for her friend, Quinn would still be wallowing in her 'hovel of filth.' In fact, she still was. She threw back the quilt and winced. "That smell is me, isn't it?"

With her lips in a grim line, Sabrina nodded again. "Yes, ma'am. It is."

She rubbed her eyes. "Where's my phone?"

"Over there. You have a ton of messages on it. The hockey moms are hungry bishes. They want Quinn-cakes and they want 'em *now*."

She arched a brow.

"I glanced at the screen while I was silencing the damn thing. If you weren't going to pick up, I wasn't going to listen to that stupid ringtone for a moment longer."

"That's fair."

Bre crossed her arms. "I'm not leaving this room until you're in the shower."

She smiled, heaved her aching body out of bed and shuffled to the bathroom where she flipped the shower on. "Water's running."

"Uh-huh. And standing next to it won't wash away that filth or those moods. Get in. I'll pick up this pile of granola bar wrappers before a family of mice decides your room is their new home."

The water wouldn't cure her of her sads. It wouldn't make her feel any less shitty for everything that had gone on between her and Will, nor would it kick her in the ass to do what she needed to do to get herself figured out.

But it would be a start. No one liked a smelly business woman. And Sabrina was right, as much as she yearned to be by herself, she couldn't spend the rest of her life buried under a duvet.

So she stepped under the steaming jets of water and tipped her head back. It was time to come up with a plan: for school, for the shelter, for her cupcakes, and for William. Because her heart hurt too damn badly to just walk away from the beautiful soul with intoxicating brown eyes.

She needed to get him back.

CHAPTER 17

Will

"Wanna talk about it?" Finn's quiet voice made him drop his spoon. It landed on the table with a clang echoing in the silence. "Must be serious." Finn jerked his chin at the half empty Tupperware container on the counter in front of Will.

Will quirked a questioning eyebrow but didn't speak. He'd done everything in his power to create space between him and Molly and Finn over the past couple of months. But this was the first time they'd been alone together since before the fateful barbecue when he'd found Finn buried in Molly's—

"You've been here at the parentals a lot this week – that's usually a sign you're stressed the hell out." Finn extended his thumb. "You're nearly done with Mama Mo's potato salad and there's already two empty Tupperware containers in the sink." He extended his index finger, counting off Will's infractions.

Will nodded. "Mac and cheese and watermelon salad."

Finn clasped both hands over his chest. "You wound me, William." He shook his head. "You know that's my favorite!

You didn't show at Applebee's for the Snow Pirates dinner the other night." His middle finger flipped out next.

"If you're just here to list my crimes, you can go. I already know them all by heart."

Finn dragged out the stool next to Will's at the breakfast bar and plopped down. "I'm here because the team missed you, Will. Hell, I miss you. Something's going on with you." Finn waved his extended digits in his face.

"I know things have been weird between us lately. I know you've been keeping your distance, but I still know you. Comfort food instead of vegetables, dropping responsibilities, no plans to do anything or go anywhere, and seeking validation from your parents? All classic Will-stress signs."

He smiled and shook his head. "I hate that you know me so well, man. I truly do."

"I'm not the only one. Mom called me. Said you've been propping up her new breakfast bar emptying her fridge every day this week. Said you had a girlfriend." Finn's side-eye game was on point. "Said you might have broken up with the girlfriend."

He shoveled another mouthful of potato salad into his face to stop words from spilling from his mouth. The heat of Finn's stare warmed the side of his face, but he refused to turn and meet his eyes.

"Auzzy said his dad granted Quinn her startup loan."

That got his attention. He couldn't fight the pride welling in his chest, or the smile on his face.

But the cracks in his heart deepened with the familiar ache that had plagued him for an entire week. He missed her.

Finn grabbed a fork and a couple of cold beers. He handed one to Will before taking his seat. "I figured you could use a friend, brother." Finn elbowed him. "So I'm just gonna sit here and share your snacks until you're ready to talk." He slid the tub of potato salad closer and took a heaped forkful.

Will's mind raced. His leg jittered under the breakfast bar. The walls closed in on him while he watched Finn shovel creamy deliciousness into his mouth and make appreciative noises that sounded like he was making out with the goddamn potatoes.

He stopped his foot from bouncing, and focused on his breathing, trying to get his shit together.

They'd moved on to their second beer and the oversized container of chicken and bacon ranch pasta salad from the fridge before either of them spoke again.

He heaved a sigh but it didn't release any of the tension held in his muscles. "Right before I met you I was sexually assaulted by one of my teachers."

Finn coughed, choking on a piece of twisted pasta. Thumping his fist against his chest, he turned wide, watering eyes to Will. "What the fuck?"

Finn's gaze darted back and forth over his face, like he was searching for some sign that Will was yanking his chain. "You didn't say anything." He slammed his mouth shut and gestured for Will to keep talking.

"In short, my..." He cringed. "Overprotective nature when it comes to Molly was pretty much coming from an extremely fucked up place of trying to keep her safe from predators. I didn't want what happened to me to happen to her."

Finn's cheek twitched, and his jaw worked from side to side, but he stayed silent. His frown deepened, and he clutched the fork in his hand so hard that his knuckles turned white.

Will scooted back his stool a few inches, just in case Finn exploded.

They sat in smothering silence for what felt like an eternity before Finn spoke again. "I don't know what to say." His voice was hoarse, misery hung from every word as he blinked back tears. "What do you need? What can I do?"

The tangled mess of knots in Will's chest loosened. He swallowed down the lump jammed in his throat and took a sip of beer. "I'm not really sure. I know I need to talk to someone... professional. I just..." He shrugged. Hot tears trickled down his cheeks.

Finn was out of his seat in an instant, wrapping his arms around Will and pulling him to his chest. "I've got you. Just let it out. I've got you."

His shoulders shook with sobs, but Finn didn't move. He held him, speaking quietly into his ear. "Whatever you need, I'm here."

Finn's words only made him sob harder. Years of repressed pain burst from behind the dam in his chest and onto his best friend's shoulder. "I'm s-so s-s-sorry, Finn."

Finn's grip tightened.

"You have no idea how much you held me together after we met." Another wave of tears rattled through him. "You saved me." He sniffed. "When you got together with Molly I... I th-thought I'd lose you to her." His voice was barely a whisper. "And I need you. I can't lose you."

He felt like a little boy again. No matter how much he wanted to fight against the vulnerability spilling from him, he knew it needed to come out. Finn needed to understand why Will reacted the way he did. He needed him to understand. He needed him to truly forgive him so they could move forward.

"Never, man. Never. I love you." Finn's body shook with sobs of his own. "I'm sorry too. I should have known there was something else going on with you. I mean, you can be a jerk but..." He clutched Will so tightly he could barely breathe.

He tapped his friend's biceps and pulled back. They stared at each other in a long, heavy silence. Finn dried his tears with the heel of his hand. "Who else knows?"

"Quinn... and Austin."

At Finn's eyebrows shooting up, he hurried to explain.

"Not on purpose. It was accidental, and he doesn't know specifics, just that something went down."

Finn nodded. "Mom, Dad, and Molly?"

He dropped his gaze.

"Will, you really need to tell your parents."

"Tell us, what?"

Will turned toward Mom's voice. She stood in the doorway to the kitchen, arms pulled tightly across herself. Dad stood beside her, hugging her to his side. They both wore frowns and their faces were pale.

"Fuck. Sorry." Finn's face paled.

He patted the side of Finn's thigh and shook his head. It was time to talk. It was time to tell his parents about the demons that had haunted him for so long. It wasn't going to be easy. He was already coming apart at the seams, but maybe once he'd gotten it off his chest to the people he loved he could figure out a better way.

One that wasn't quite so crippling.

"You're making me nervous, Willy. What's wrong?" Molly sat on the edge of their parents' couch, hands clasped on her lap. "Are you sick?"

Finn had offered to sit next to Molly while Will talked to her, but he wanted to do it alone – he needed to do it alone.

"Will?"

He took a deep breath before crouching in front of her and taking her hands in his. "I'm not sick. But I need to tell you about some things that happened." He shook his head, unsure of where to start. "I'm sorry I was so controlling and overprotective of you."

She huffed out a small laugh. "You've already apologized,

and I've already forgiven you, silly." She shoved his shoulder and he rocked back on his heels.

"There's a reason I was so controlling and..." He swallowed against the bitter taste rising in his throat. "Judgmental. It's not because I don't love you."

She nodded. "I know you do. And things with me and Finn, we'll figure out our new normal, I know we will. I have no doubts."

He couldn't help but smile at her insistence they'd all be okay, her unwavering belief in the three of them making it through.

"I was..." The words jammed in his throat. He rolled his eyes to the ceiling in an attempt to blink back the tears threatening to fall once again. "I was... uh... inappropriately touched by a teacher in high school, Molly. And I've spent..." He stumbled over his tongue and raked his hand over his jaw.

She stiffened, and her eyes went wide.

"I spent the years after trying to protect you from ever being violated the way I was." Stroking the back of her hand with his thumb, he couldn't look at her. "I know I went about it the wrong way. I know it was unhealthy and overbearing and just plain insulting."

A hiccupping sob escaped him. "And I'm so fucking sorry I ever made you feel the way I did."

She launched herself at him, throwing her arms around his neck and sending him off balance. Her eyes narrowed, turning cold as her nostrils flared. "Who hurt you, Willy?" She gave him a beat to reply before charging ahead. "I mean it. I will end him, whoever he is."

"She."

Her jaw dropped.

"I know. Everyone expects sexual assailants to be men, but women hurt people too."

She nodded. "No, I know. I just... I can't believe it." Her

spine steeled in front of him. "Whatever you need, we've got you, you know that, right? We're here."

"I know. Thank you. I need to go see someone. A therapist. Someone qualified to help me figure out what to do with this baggage."

"I'm proud of you, Will. So fucking proud."

She should be mad at him, disappointed, angry, hurt, and hell, she was probably a combination of all those things, but she still found it in her to tell him she was proud of him. He didn't deserve her kindness, but he sure as shit needed it.

She hugged him again and when she pulled back, her face had changed, hardened. Shit. He was about to get hit with something but his brain couldn't figure out what.

"What did you do to fuck things up with Quinn?" She pushed his shoulder again. "I like her. You can't just let her go."

He scratched the back of his neck.

"Ah ha. Guilty Willy. That tells me all I need to know. You were a dick, weren't you?" She pointed an accusatory finger at him.

"I might have said some things... but she was a bit full on."

"Did you tell her that and ask for space?"

He shook his head.

"From what I hear – and I'm paraphrasing here – you told her she was a terrible human being."

He took a step back. "I did not."

"Uh. Yeah. You totally did. Telling her she was judgmental and self-righteous? That's basically the same thing to someone like Quinn."

He folded his arms. "And you're suddenly an expert on my girlfriend?" He winced. "Ex-girlfriend."

She grinned. "No, but I'm one of the Snow Pirates' girlfriends now. We hang out, we talk, we drink together. Sabrina can't hold her liquor. She's a sweet girl, and she's worried about her friend."

She sat on the couch and patted the sofa cushion next to her.

"She says Quinn has barely left her bedroom in a week."

His heart sank as his chest deflated. His poor Starburst.

"She loves you, Willy. And from the look of sheer agony on your face right now, you love her too."

He nodded.

"Then we gotta get her back. What d'ya got?"

He bolted to his feet and paced back and forth, mulling things over in his head for a minute. "I have something, but... it's... big..."

"Big works."

"It'll take some planning... a real team effort... On second thought, it might be too big."

"Too big for the Morrisons? For the championship winning Snow Pirates? " Finn clapped his hands together as he walked into the living room. "Bullshit. There ain't no such thing, sunshine. Let's win back your girl."

"William Morrison?"

He stood up from the chair in the psychologist's waiting room and raised his hand. "It's eh, just Will, actually."

"Follow me, Will."

The doctor towered over Will as he made his way past him and into the office.

"Take a seat." He gestured to the empty chair across the table with his clipboard as he sat down. "My name is Amos King. What brought you in here today?"

Will stretched an open hand across the desk. "Dr. King, it's a pleasure to meet you. Thank you for seeing me." He paused, then laughed.

"Yeah. Just call me Amos." The giant chuckled. How the man wasn't a defensive tackle for the Minnesota Vikings was anyone's guess.

He sat and took in the room. Rich, dark wood book-shelves filled with textbooks and a picture of Amos at his grad-uation. Framed diplomas hung to the left. A large window with emerald green drapes let in the high morning sun to his right.

He swallowed, reminding himself he couldn't start to heal unless he opened up and let Amos in. He'd shared with his best friend, his parents, his sister, and some of his teammates, they were all there for him if he needed them. He probably did, but he didn't know what he needed. Amos would help with that.

Or at least, he would if Will opened his mouth and spat out the words burning his tongue. "In high school I was sexu-ally assaulted by my English teacher."

Amos remained quiet and still. He didn't write anything on the notebook resting on his crossed legs, and his face didn't display a single trace of pity.

"She didn't rape me or anything. But she kissed me... touched me..." He closed his eyes and sucked in a deep breath, battling the emotions stirring in his chest at the memories and the overwhelming guilt clawing at him.

When he opened his eyes, he released a breath. "I wasn't the only one either."

Amos folded his hands on top of the notebook. "How long have you kept that to yourself?"

"Seven or eight years, maybe? I... I'm not sure."

"Have you told anyone else?"

He nodded. "I told my best friend, my parents, and my

sister a couple days ago. But it's not enough." He rubbed at his chest. "I've been reacting really terribly to my sister over the past year. She's grown up." He scrunched up his face.

"You got over protective?"

He nodded. "It all came to a head when I caught her and my best friend, Finn, together. *Together* together, y'know? I said some things…" He fell quiet.

"Have you told any of them the details?"

"No."

"Have you seen the person again since?"

"I saw her at a fundraiser a while back. I guess it was the catalyst for me being here. Seeing her… well, it brought up a lot of stuff I've been really struggling to deal with since."

"Okay." Amos put the cap on his pen and placed it on the desk. "I'd like for you to take me back to high school, and tell me every detail you can remember about each and every instance with her. It's not going to be easy, and it's going to hurt like hell, but I'm going to ask you to trust me. And I'm going to remind you that I'm here with you every step, okay?"

He nodded again but his stomach was sour. Why had he made the appointment again?

"I know it's a lot. You're here with a complete stranger. You're expected to just pour out your suffering, show your vulnerabilities, and let me in."

It was as though Amos was reading his mind. "It can be daunting, Will. And it's going to be a hell of a lot of hard work. But you came here for help. And I can help you. The question is, will you let me?"

CHAPTER 18
Quinn

Another week had passed, but instead of being a sobbing, depressive mess under a blanket surrounded by her own stink and empty *Nature Valley* wrappers and *Cheez-it* boxes, she'd been back at school.

She'd almost caught up on all the shit she'd missed, too.

She'd met with Austin and his not-nearly-as-scary-as-she'd-expected accountant. They'd talked her through the fine print of getting a startup business loan from Daddy Morgan – whose pockets ran so deep he didn't care to meet her himself.

She wasn't sure whether to be offended at his seeming disinterest or impressed with Austin. He obviously had his father's trust and was choosing to use his superpowers for good. That was something she could get behind.

She'd also taken on board two more birthday party orders from the hockey moms. Nova hadn't been shy about sharing Quinn's digits with her friends, and despite her self-doubts, Quinn was excited to see what she could come up with in the kitchen.

Sabrina had been underfoot all week, making sure Quinn drank her water and ate something unprocessed that grew outside in nature, and ensuring she didn't succumb to the allure of the safety and comfort of her bed.

She had to admit, it was tempting.

Her heart felt like it had been squeezed through a vise – twice over – then through a shredder for good measure. She'd walked into the Sugar Bean during the week, spotted the back of Will's head as he sat with some of his hockey buds, spun on her heel and literally ran the other way.

She hardly ever ran. The only time she would run is if a t-rex was chasing her. And apparently when she saw William Morrison, post-breakup. It was very mature of her.

But she couldn't stand the idea of facing him, of seeing him happy, of, well, seeing him *period*.

As if on cue, her heart fluttered. She missed him. His lazy, lopsided smile. His cognac eyes that she could get lost in. His fit and lean body with a lil squish developing in the middle from not training every single day. She missed his affection, his kisses, that thing he did with his tongue...

She sighed. It was 5PM on Friday evening and she was already in her favorite *Star Trek* tee. She had worn it so often that it was no longer fit for public consumption. She'd paired it with a pair of pink pj shorts and oversized furry socks that came up to her knee. Fashionistas beware: Quinn was in the house.

She was parked on the couch in front of the TV, pint of Ben and Jerry's in hand, watching *Star Trek Voyager* and reciting all the lines a split second before the actors. She sure knew how to live life to the fullest.

Stabbing her spoon into the ice cream, she stood. She needed to shake off the break-up funk and figure out a way to move forward.

So Will wasn't the book boyfriend dreams were made of like she'd thought. So what? There were plenty more potential suitors in the sea.

Except he was, and she'd fucked it all up by being a meddling meddler.

She jabbed at the ice cream again before taking a heaped spoon and sliding it onto her tongue. If there was a more delicious flavor of ice cream than mint choc chip she'd eat her hat.

The door to the apartment burst open and Sabrina skipped in, dress bag in each hand and a broad grin on her face. She paused, her eyes widened – probably at how downright sexy Quinn looked in her nighttime getup – and shook her head.

"Shower. Now." Sabrina jerked her head toward the bathroom.

She waved her spoon. "Don't you judge me. Can't you be more like Ben and Jerry? They are very accepting guys, they don't require formal wear to keep me company while I binge watch *Star Trek*."

Sabrina hung the dress bags on the door frame. "Look. We don't have a lot of time, and I don't have a lot of details so don't ask." She pursed her lips. "Just work with me, okay?"

She put the ice cream away before spinning to face her friend. "What did you do?"

"You trust me, right?"

"Ride or die."

"Then no questions. Get in the shower, make your hair do that pretty loose curl thing it does and put on some sparkly green eyeshadow when you do your make up."

She opened her mouth to ask what the fuck was going on.

"Ah." Bre held a finger to her own lips. "Shh. No questions. No time. Just…" Sabrina waved a hand at Quinn's face. "Fix that."

She snorted. She'd play along, but she wouldn't defuzz for her.

Just as she turned on the shower, Sabrina's voice echoed around the bathroom. "And don't forget to shave – I want you silky smooth all over, Quinny. Put some effort in. Use the good body scrub, too."

Was Bre taking her out on a date? Why did she need to be clean shaven? She growled. "I hate you right now."

"Lies. You love me. And I love you too. Which is why I'm not letting you wallow away another weekend. Be quick!"

Wasting no time, she showered, shaved, moisturized, and curled her hair with the fancy wand thing Sabrina had given her two Christmases ago. It looked like anal beads on a stick but it got the job done. She was flicking out her eyeliner in the bedroom mirror when Bre entered.

She gasped. "Bre. You look stunning."

Sabrina wore an orange and gold saree with red floral accents. Her thick black hair had been put in a simple twist. She'd accessorized with gold drop earrings, bangles, and a large ring on the middle finger of her right hand with red accents that matched the delicate thread in the saree.

"Where the hell are we going? A wedding? I don't have anything like... that..." Her jaw hung open. Her friend was breathtaking. "You need to make sure Russ doesn't see you until you get where you're going or he's gonna..." She made a circle with her thumb and finger and slid the forefinger of her other hand through the hole.

"You're disgusting."

"And also correct. Girl. I'm straight and even I wanna do you right now."

Despite Sabrina's darker skin, the blush painting her cheeks was obvious. "It's a special night."

Another gasp. "Did I forget something? Parent's anniversary? A wedding? What the hell is going on?"

Bre giggled and shook her head. "Trust me. And quit asking questions; you're going to ruin the surprise." She popped her eyes wide like she'd said something she shouldn't have. "Your dress is in the living room. Wear your good underwear."

Like it made a difference what underwear she should wear when it was only her who'd see it. "So no period panties?"

Sabrina glared. "No period panties. Hurry up, they'll be here soon." Another wide-eyed pause. "Shit. Just... move faster."

She waved the wand of her eye liner. "Either you want my wings to match or you want them done fast. What's it going to be?"

"You can flick those wings with your eyes closed and one hand tied behind your back, Quinny. Stop stalling. Move it."

Ten minutes later, she tugged the zipper of the dress bag hanging from the wooden doorframe. Her breath caught as the black cover gave way to beautiful emerald green fabric. "Oh my god, Bre this is..." She traced her fingers over the soft material.

A sweetheart neckline with off the shoulder straps. The whole torso of the dress was covered with an intricate lace overlay that spread over to the top part of the full bodied satin skirt.

"Sabrina..." Her voice was a whisper. "I can't wear this. This is... Wow."

"You can and you will. With your pale skin and your red hair... You're going to look like an Irish goddess." She pulled out her phone while Quinn slid the dress from the hanger and opened the zipper.

She eased the silky fabric over her head and slipped her arms through the delicate straps that sat mid-way down her biceps. "Where the hell are we going?" She clutched the front of the dress and presented Sabrina with her bare back.

"Bre?"

"Sorry, I was looking up Irish goddesses. Your picture is

right there next to the phrase." Sabrina zipped up the dress. "Turn."

When she spun to face her, Sabrina beamed. She clapped her hands together. "Perfect. You look beautiful Quinny. Let's take a selfie."

Still clueless as to what the hell was happening, Quinn shuffled forward and nestled herself against Sabrina's side while she snapped some pictures. Why was one selfie never enough? Why did it take 3,718 different takes and 800 different positions to find one single acceptable photo of two attractive women?

"I shaved for you."

"It'll be worth it. Promise." Bre brushed her lips against Quinn's cheeks. "Get your shoes on. The silver ones that criss-cross in front."

She pursed her lips. "You sure I shouldn't wear the ones with the higher heels."

Without a second thought, Bre shook her head. "Crisscross."

Shaking her head, she huffed out a laugh. "Yes, ma'am. You sure are bossy for someone who's keeping a giant secret from your best friend."

Sabrina made a shooing motion with her hands, and Quinn left to find her silver sandals – the ones that criss-crossed in front, because heaven forbid she go against Bre's wishes at this stage of the game.

As she fastened the buckle on her second shoe, the door-bell chimed. Whoever was coming had obviously arrived. Standing in front of the mirror she snapped a selfie on her phone and posted it to Instagram with the caption: *Bestie taking me somewhere classy AF tonight. I feel like a freakin' princess.*

The photo had barely finished uploading before she got a notification that the one and only William Morrison had liked it. Her breath stuttered. Maybe he'd accidentally hit the love heart. She'd done it herself more times than she'd cared to admit.

A second notification came through.

Will_Morrison: You look exquisite, Q.

She wouldn't cry. She wouldn't. She'd lost her favorite mascara and she didn't know if her back up was even waterproof. Did they make non-waterproof mascara anymore? She had no idea, and she wasn't going to find out by leaving black streaks down her face.

"Come on, Quinny!"

Checking her lipstick one last time, she smoothed out the satin skirt of her dress and smiled. She had no idea where the hell she was going, but she couldn't remember ever feeling so freakin' special.

In the living room, Sabrina, Cleo, and Kenzie stood sipping champagne from red solo cups while Molly slugged straight from the bottle. Bre held out a plastic cup for Quinn as she made her way to where they stood. They were all kitted out in fancy dresses, with stunning makeup and perfect hair.

What the fuck was going on?

Her confusion must have been obvious to the group. Molly cradled the end of Quinn's cup and tipped it. "Drink. You're going to need it."

She wore a red, calf-length gown. A thick satin ribbon curved around her waist above a puffy tulle skirt, while the top of the dress was sweetheart cut and sported red flowers and silver beads over the top of nude material. She had thin straps which rested on the very edge of her shoulders and her lips were the perfect shade of red to match her dress.

"You're freaking her out." Kenzie pulled a hip flask from under the skirts of her navy blue gown. The bodice was dotted with silver sparkles and flattered the fuck out of her tits. Her shoulders were bare and the two thick bands of fabric looped around her neck and crisscrossed on her back.

"You're all making me question my sexuality." She sipped from her cup before pointing it at the women surrounding her. "I'm very sexually confused right now. None of you are gonna tell me what's going on?"

"Nope." Cleo took a sip from her cup. She wore a dramatic V-neck, deep purple, floor length gown. It hugged her curves like she'd been poured into it.

Fuck she had gorgeous friends.

"Quinny?" Sabrina's frown was deep, crinkling her head and making her eyes small. "Why do you look like you're going to cry?"

"Overwhelm? I dunno. I have no idea what we're about to do, but we all look fierce as fuck and I love all you crazy bitches." She rushed them, arms wide open, and pulled them into a group hug.

Molly called time on the 'soppy shit' and demanded a series of selfies and staged pictures while they worked through their second bottle of champagne. Even if all they did for the evening was parade around her living room, Quinn was living her best life.

Almost every phone in the room chimed at the same time, like a group text had been sent to everyone but her. The girls exchanged knowing glances and an excited buzz whipped through the air.

"Let's roll, ladies. Our chariot awaits." Molly took one last pull from the bottle before placing it on the counter. She gave Quinn's shoulders a squeeze before getting in line behind Sabrina. Wait, they were getting in line? What the hell?

With a shrug, she fell in behind Kenzie, feeling short as the blonde towered over her by at least six inches. She should have worn the taller heels, damnit.

Outside, she leaned around her girls to get a look at what –

and who – was waiting for them. A stretch limo was parked next to the curb and Lincoln Scott stood, corsage in hand, waiting for Cleo at the front of what looked like a line of penguins.

The outfits, the limo, the corsages – this was like... Quinn gasped. "I never went to prom."

"This is absolutely brand new information," Molly cooed back at her.

Were they going to prom? What else could it be? Though it was almost the end of summer and not at all prom season. Maybe there was another fundraiser they were all going to. Butterflies slapped in her hungry stomach. Ice cream didn't count as real food, and she was starving.

Holy fuck. Was Will standing in the line waiting to take her to prom?

Cleo stepped forward, accepting the corsage on her wrist and linking her arm through Linc's. He led them to the limo while Russ stepped forward in line. His corsage was an orange Asiatic lily to match Sabrina's saree, but instead of putting it on her wrist, he slid it into the twist in her hair, kissed her cheek, and extended his arm to take her to the car.

Molly launched herself at Finn, looping her legs around his waist and kissing him full force. He carried her like that to the car, still clutching the box with her corsage.

Austin was next, and while he wasn't her type, she couldn't help but drool. Damn did the man fill out a tux like he was born to wear one.

Austin greeted Mackenzie with a yellow rose corsage that he slipped onto her wrist. He splayed his hand on the bare skin on Kenzie's back and kissed her, making Quinn's cheeks burn and some of their friends whistle.

But she couldn't take her eyes off the last penguin standing. "William." His name fell from her lips before she could stop it. Had he done this?

"You really do look exquisite, Q." He stepped forward, holding an emerald green and silver fake-flower corsage with black glitter in the center.

It had strands of sparkles and pearls, was finished with a black ribbon bow, and was set on an elastic pearl bracelet.

"What are you doing here?" Her lip trembled, but she'd be damned if she was going to cry.

"We need to talk."

She snorted and gestured over his shoulder. "In front of all our friends? Dressed like this?"

He shrugged. "If that's what it takes to get you back, then yes." Holding out the corsage, he reached for her arm, but waited for her nod before slipping it over her wrist.

He wanted her back. Her heart raced. "Are we really going to prom?"

Will nodded.

"You remembered our conversation from that first night at the bar that I didn't get to go?"

"I did."

"And you did... all this...?" She swept her hand toward the limo.

"Not without help." Finn had extricated his lips from Molly's for long enough to throw his two cents into the conversation.

She laughed. Their friends all lined up along the limo behind him and she fought the urge to snap a picture. They all scrubbed up well. She'd never before seen such an attractive bunch of people all in one place.

She inched toward Will. There was too much space between them. He might not have been as big as the other guys in their group, but he was still her safe space. Every molecule in her body ached to touch him, and to have him touch her.

"I'm sorry."

"I'm sorry."

They both spoke at the same time, then laughed. Her cheeks heated. His turned pink.

All eyes were on them. Each of the women stood in front of their penguin, and Molly clasped her hands under her chin, her eyes glistening as she shamelessly eavesdropped.

"You go first."

"You go first."

Another laugh.

"I'm sorry I said what I said to you. I was angry."

Before she could answer, he hurried ahead. "Not at you, at myself, at the world... Everything was just bubbling up inside me and I didn't know what to do with it. Lashing out at you... saying things I didn't mean... that wasn't okay."

His gaze met hers as he held her hands in his. "I'm so sorry. I started therapy a couple weeks ago. I'm going multiple times a week. It's hard as hell." He blinked rapidly but tears still escaped from the corners of his eyes. "I miss you, Q. I want you back."

She smiled at his straightforward words. He was never one to beat around the bush and she liked when he told it how it was.

"I miss you, too, William. I'm sorry I pressured you to talk about everything before you were ready. You were right, I should have known better. I just get carried away sometimes and—"

His soft lips were on hers before she could take a breath. Threading her hands into his hair she held him against her while their friends whooped and cheered. He pulled back before she was ready and extended his hand to her. "Come on, Starburst. We have a prom to go to."

CHAPTER 19

Quinn

They paused for a few group photos in front of the limo before they all clambered inside. The interior of the car was black leather with silver accents. There were fridges with bottles of champagne, plastic flute glasses, and lights strung around the ceiling that changed color every few minutes.

Will pulled her onto his lap as the car spluttered to life and pulled away from the curb. Cleo handed out glasses of fizz, while Kenzie and Molly snapped pictures of everyone, some candid, some posed.

"I can't believe you did this." Quinn stroked Will's jaw with the side of her thumb as she rested her forehead against his.

"I didn't do it alone. In case you were unaware, party planning is not one of my strengths."

"Molly?"

He nodded, and she scanned their friends around the limo. Molly was already staring at her, her brows pressed together in a small frown. Quinn mouthed "thank you" and her expression softened.

"Where are we going? No one told me anything about anything."

He rubbed his nose against hers. "Pippa was only too happy to let us use the community center hall where you held the auction. Everyone had to buy tickets and the money is all going to the shelter."

Tears welled in her eyes as she buried her face into his shoulder. "William!"

His hands tightened around her waist as they fell into silence. There was so much she needed to say, so many things to thank him for, but she couldn't find the words.

"I love you, Q. It's been a while since I told you that and I really don't want to give you the chance to forget it."

Stick a fork in her, she was done. "I love you, too, William."

A few minutes later, they arrived at the shelter. Pippa stood in front of the double doors to the hall like a glamorous security guard. She wore a cotton candy pink halter gown with a slit all the way up to her mid-thigh. She twirled in a circle as soon as Quinn got close.

"Not bad for an old lady, right?"

She snorted. "You make it sound like you're a hundred years old, Pippa. You're in your forties for fuck's sake."

"Ah. Ah." Pippa wagged a finger. "You don't get to look like that and talk like that."

She shook her head. "You're not my mama. And you cuss way more than I do."

"Elders' prerogative."

"Turn around, Q. Let me get a photo of you with Pippa." Will held his phone ready to take a picture, but Nova appeared in a slinky gold backless dress, cradling a professional camera.

"I got this one, Will. But don't go too far, I want one of you and Quinn, too. I'm getting one of each of the couples, then the whole team, then the girls, then the whole group..."

She paused to suck in a deep breath and throw a grin at Quinn. "I'm nervous."

No shit. Was she also on drugs? No human being could talk that fast.

Nova glanced over her shoulder. "I'm on a date."

"With one of the Snow Pirates?" Her jaw dropped.

"No, silly. I met a guy online. He didn't run when I told him I was a single mama and he looks hot as fuck in a tuxedo." She waggled her eyebrows. "Betchurass I'm getting me a lil somethin' somethin' tonight, girlfriend. No vibrators for me this weekend."

Will coughed, his face turning as red as his sister's dress as Nova clicked her camera, taking pictures of her and Pippa.

"This is surreal." She shook her head.

"Wait till you get in there." Nova jerked her thumb at the door. "They pulled out all the stops. Even their coach is here. Not bad for a last minute shindig. Your boy done good."

Her eyes bugged wide. "Coach Swift is here? Does that mean we have to behave?"

Will chuckled and started to speak, but Kenzie grabbed her by her elbow. "He's here on a date. With my freakin' neighbor, Clare. Can you believe it? My boss and my neighbor? I had grand plans to get shit-faced tonight. But I guess I gotta stay responsible now." She rolled her eyes, but smiled.

Clearly she wasn't in the least bit upset by the events unfolding. She dug under her skirt and pulled out a hip flask.

"Where the hell are you keeping that?"

"It's best not to ask." Kenzie took a mouthful from the silver flask and offered it to her. "I feel so fancy."

Quinn looked up at the curvy goddess standing next to her and accepted the flask. "Aren't you like a pageant queen or something?"

Kenzie nodded. "Sure. But everythin's different when you have someone lookin' at you like that." She jerked her chin at

Austin who – sure enough – was eyeing her like he was a drowning man and she was oxygen. "And that." She inclined her head toward Will.

His eyes were hungry and filled with a love she'd never known. He looked at her like no man ever had. It took her breath away.

She pressed her palm to her diaphragm. "Wow." Clearing her throat, she turned back to Kenzie, her face on fire. "Yeah. Okay. I get it."

Kenzie laughed, throwing her head back, the tiny blue stud in her nose glinting in the light.

Behind her, someone clapped their hands, and she turned to find Will beaming. "Okay guys, we should probably go inside, but I wanted to just take a minute..." His Adam's apple bobbed, and he paused, surveying the group.

"I just wanted to say... I..." He paused again and swallowed. "Just... Thank you all."

From the sincerity in his voice, she got the feeling he wasn't just talking about prom, but that was all he said. His eyes glistened, and he nodded like he was convincing himself he was okay.

Finn broke the silence by jerking the doors open, and Will slipped his hand into hers, leading her into a magical room of twinkling lights and swaying bodies. A band was already set up on stage, with the singer blasting out *Isn't She Lovely* by Stevie Wonder.

"You're kidding me."

"I couldn't throw you a prom and have some contemporary band pumping out tunes you wouldn't dance to now, could I?"

"They're going to play classics? All night?"

"All night." Will looked so proud of himself, and she couldn't blame him. She tugged him toward the dance floor.

Linking her hands at the nape of his neck, her hips were already swaying. "What else can they play?"

"Motown, disco, soul... all that old shit you and my parents love." He winked at her.

"You know I love the classics."

"They're going to throw in some modern stuff for those of us who aren't old souls, but this night is all about you so..."

Stunned into silence, she leaned into the warmth of his palms on her waist and pulled him closer, taking the opportunity to look at the rest of the dancefloor over his shoulder.

There were at least a hundred people and she only knew a fraction of them. Mr. and Mrs. Morrison stood at the edge of the dancefloor chatting to another couple. The man bore a striking resemblance to Austin from the side.

Wow. From all reports Mr. Morgan wasn't exactly the kind of man who busted a groove with his son at a fundraiser, but maybe he was changing. They were all changing.

She couldn't believe the work Will had put into the evening. He had even convinced his friends to invite their parents. And how the hell had they pulled together such an impressive event with such short notice?

As though reading her thoughts, he swept a kiss across her forehead. "Snow Pirates get shit done."

"That's got to be your new slogan." She laughed. "And you can be smug all you want, William. This is impressive as hell. I don't think I could have pulled this off, and I love planning parties. Who are all these people?"

Will pulled back enough to look at her face. "Friends, families, survivors... The Snow Pirates have back to back games starting tomorrow." He shrugged. "I might have made some calls to some of my friends on the visiting teams and asked if they wanted to treat their other halves to a night on the town."

Her eyes flexed wide. "So... we're dancing with..." She looked over both shoulders. "The enemy?"

"Yup. Mustangs tomorrow night, and Raccoons the next. Those who are single or whose girlfriends couldn't afford to make the last minute trip across the country – cause let's face it, it's not cheap. Well, we paired them up with the survivors at the shelter who wanted to come along for the night."

Holy shit. She couldn't breathe. Emotion clogged her throat as she rasped out his name.

"Shhhhh." He inched closer to her.

"I can't believe you did all of this for me."

"Well, you... and the shelter."

Tears threatened to ruin her makeup, so she bit down on the inside of her cheek and swayed as the music changed to *Baby Love* by the Supremes. It was going to be a great night.

"Quite the soiree you put together here, Mo." To her left, a guy she didn't quite recognize swayed with a beautiful brunette in his arms. He tipped his head at Quinn. "Aren't you going to introduce us to your good lady?"

Will's sigh was almost as dramatic as his eye roll. "Quinn, this is Jeremy Lewis from the Alabama Mustangs. Perpetual pain in our ass, thorn in our side..."

"What he *means* to say is: epically talented, devilishly handsome, and always down to a par-tay for a great cause."

"Or on days ending in 'Y.'" The brunette supplied an eye roll of her own. "Chelsea." She stuck her hand out and Quinn accepted it with a shake.

"Quinn. Thanks for traveling all the way up here for this. It really means a lot to me... and the shelter."

"He threatened us all with physical violence if we didn't." Jeremy's face was solemn, but his eyes sparkled with mischief under the giant disco ball spinning overhead.

"Sounds like him. It's the only reason you'd dance with the enemy, right?"

"That... and those tasty AF cupcakes over there. I've already hidden two for later."

"And that's on top of the three he thought no one saw him shoving in his pie hole." Chelsea smirked.

As they moved away, she snorted, trying to locate the dessert table at the edge of the room. "Dare I ask where you got your baked goods from?"

His lips twitched, and he pointed at her. "From you."

She gasped. "You did not!"

"Did too. You made an order of ten dozen cupcakes for a hockey mom yesterday."

Her jaw dropped. "How did you know that?"

His body shook with silent laughter. "Spoiler alert: I'm the hockey mom."

"I thought she just really liked cake and had a huge family or something." She couldn't help but laugh. "Or maybe she was PMS-ing, hard. I eat a *lot* of cake before my period."

"I wouldn't go to anyone else in the city for desserts now that I've tried yours."

"That's the sweetest thing you've ever said to me." She brushed her lips over his and gagging noises got louder to his right.

"Timeout on the sucking face with my big bro for a second please." Molly stood with her hands in a 'T' shape with Finn over her shoulder. "I hear you're opening a new bakery, Quinn. I have a new product idea for you."

Oh. This was going to be good. She twitched her eyebrows to indicate Molly should keep talking.

"I want to be able to order a giant cookie. And it needs to come in a box, right?"

She was with her so far.

"Once you open the box there needs to be a card that says something like, 'Have a cookie and stop running your fucking mouth.'"

Finn stepped forward, but Molly held out a hand. "Like

you can't think of at least half a dozen people you'd send a STFU cookie to."

Finn raised his eyebrows like she had a point.

"I have a bunch of ideas. I mean, they're all profanity based, obviously."

Will smirked. "Obviously."

"But we should definitely talk."

Quinn laughed. "Sure. I'd like that."

"See, Willy." Molly shoved Will's shoulder. "She'd like that."

She was the most beautiful girl in the room and she was looking at him like he'd hung the damn moon. Had putting together a prom with just over a week's notice been easy? No. Had they made it work? Sure, it was what they did. Was it worth it? Every last second of blood, sweat, and tears, a million times over.

He'd been surprised at the eagerness of the visiting teams to step up and help out. One of the Cedar Rapids Raccoons had a hook up to the band – which was just as well as he wouldn't have had the first idea where to find a band to play all the golden oldies she loved so much.

The two teams had also done a whip round among those who couldn't attend the event and come up with a tidy sum for donation to the shelter. The kicker was, whatever the Snow Pirates raised to donate, Austin's dad was matching. Quinn would lose her mind.

Even the coaching staff from the visiting teams had dusted off their tuxes to join the festivities. Coach Swift stood at the side of the dancefloor in animated conversation with the other two head coaches while their dates chatted next to the punch fountain.

Everything was perfect. Especially his girl. Having her back in his arms felt as right as hot cocoa and marshmallows, Tuesdays and Tacos, RuPaul and drag.

He would never let her go again.

"Will?" Quinn was clearly waiting for an answer to a question he hadn't heard. She turned her head and mouthed, "Austin."

"Austin, hey. Sorry. I was in a world of my own."

"I am sorry to interrupt. But I just spoke with Fath—uh… my dad and he had one condition for granting the investment for the First Mates."

"Okay?" He let go of Quinn and turned to face his friend who pointed straight at Will's chest.

"You. He wants you to be their permanent coach."

Quinn hissed out a "yessssss" while Austin's words filtered through his brain.

"C-can he do that? What about a fair interview process…?"

Austin shook his head. "The position has been open for the guts of a year, Will. The kids deserve a committed, talented, and invested coach who will not leave them from game to game."

"Coaching won't take away from time helping you out at the bakery." Will nudged Quinn with his hip.

"If you don't say yes I'm going to make Austin punch you. And that'll get blood on your nice white shirt." She planted her hands on her hips and tilted her chin as if to say 'try me.'

"You're savage."

"Aggressively supportive."

"Okay." He nodded. "I'm in."

Austin shook his hand and suggested they get together the following week to talk through the finer details, but to all intents and purposes he was officially the head coach of the First Mates. It felt kinda great.

No sooner had Austin left them to their dance than Mom and Dad appeared next to him and Quinn. And while Will ached for some alone time with his girlfriend, he couldn't begrudge Dad's outstretched hand and Quinn's wide smile as she slipped her hand in his.

She never spoke about her parents, and he wouldn't push her to, but he loved seeing how quickly his brought her into the fold.

"You did a good thing here, Will." Mom swayed in his arms as the band sang *Say a Little Prayer for You*.

"We all did. She's worth it. So's Pippa's Place."

"I love how happy she makes you. You're going to do great things together."

With Quinn by his side, he could take over the world without breaking a sweat. "Austin's dad is going to invest in the junior hockey team. He wants me at the helm, coaching the kids."

She lowered her mouth to his ear. "I know. He just told us. Congratulations, son. We couldn't be prouder."

He didn't realize how much he needed to hear Mom's validation of his life choices until she'd said the words. He nodded, but didn't speak.

"This band is fantastic." The music shifted once again and the drum solo at the start of *Easy Lover* by Phil Collins echoed around the room. "Quinn has great taste."

Pippa had stolen Quinn from Dad, so Dad rescued Mom from his poor attempts at dancing. Pippa, Quinn, and Kenzie stood together in a cluster dancing around what had to be Pippa's bright pink purse. Pippa and Quinn pointed at each other, and their shout-singing could just about be heard over the music.

When he caught her eye, she wiggled her head from side to

side and kept singing at him, her auburn waves jostling around her shoulders.

Warmth expanded in his chest at the sight of her hips swaying and her wide grin lighting up the room. He was the luckiest guy in the fucking world.

"Luckiest guy in the world, right?" Finn stepped up beside him and held out a bottle of beer for Will.

He took it, clinked it against the neck of Finn's bottle, and nodded. "Damn straight."

"I'm proud of you, man." Finn bumped shoulders with him while his eyes stayed firmly pinned on his girl.

"Thanks. I think I might be proud of me, too."

"About fucking time. Oh shit. Put down your drink. Let's go." Finn swiped his bottle before he'd even taken a drink and dragged him onto the floor.

The Snow Pirates' women were all sitting on the floor, one behind the other. Mom, Russ's mom Natalie, Pippa, and the coach's dates were all joining the line.

Most of the Snow Pirates mirrored the line as *Rock the Boat* blasted from the speakers. The girls wasted no time clapping the floor to their left, clapping in front of their chests, and clapping the ground to their right.

Quinn raised her eyebrows like he was a complete idiot and mouthed at him to hurry up. When seated, half of the pirates went left while the other went right and the collective eye roll and head shake of the women made him burst out laughing.

Molly disconnected herself from the women and stood at the front of the men's line, yelling commands. If anyone could whip them into shape it was her.

By the end of the night, his feet hurt from dancing, his ribs and cheeks hurt from laughing and his stomach and heart were full.

"Tired?" Quinn laced her fingers in his as he led her up to his apartment.

He nodded through a yawn.

"*Too* tired?"

He grabbed her hips and pressed his semi against her ass. "Never."

CHAPTER 20

Quinn

No one had ever before done anything for her like Will had. He'd not only given her an experience she had missed out on in high school, but he'd done it in aid of a cause close to her heart – and his.

She was so fucking proud of him. And so fucking grateful.

They'd raised thousands for the shelter – thou-sands. On the ride home, Molly had let it slip that Daddy Moneybags – aka Mr. Morgan – was dollar-for-dollar matching the Snow Pirates total raised.

She'd almost shit herself right then and there on Will's lap. Pippa was going to lose her fucking mind when she found out. She'd last been seen behind the punch table, making out with someone who strongly resembled the equipment manager for the Snow Pirates.

Quinn would need to burn the image out of her mind with acid or bleach.

She couldn't wait to tell her. Pippa's Place was her whole life, she poured her soul into her work and Quinn was thrilled to have spread the word to people who had some real influence, and deep pockets, at last.

As she led Will up to his apartment, she couldn't help but look back over her shoulder. Her life had changed so dramatically since she'd met him that day in the bookstore, and she had a hard time remembering how it had been without him.

"What?"

"What, what?" She scrunched up her face.

"You're staring."

"You're easy to stare at, William. Especially in that penguin suit."

His eyebrows peaked as he tilted his head.

Sighing, she shrugged. "I was just thinking how much my life has changed since I met you. And I really can't believe everything you did for me tonight."

It was Will's turn to shrug. "I'd do anything for you."

He said it like it was no big deal. And if she hadn't been standing in the hallway outside his apartment, she'd have dropped to her knees and worshiped at the shrine of the dick of Morrison. How was he so humble, so kind, and so goddamn genuine?

"You take my breath away sometimes. You know that, right?"

He twisted the key in the lock and pushed the door open, letting her enter first. "I guess that makes us even for all the times you take my breath away. Like tonight. In that dress. You're like a vision, Q."

He kicked the door closed with the tip of his foot and took her hand, twirling her under his arm. "I had the most beautiful girl in the room by my side for the evening." Another twirl. "And you know, I don't think she even realizes how spectacular she truly is."

As much as she struggled accepting compliments, it was hard not to get swept up in his enthusiasm as he stared at her with such affection.

"Hardworking." He swept a stray curl from her face. "Conscientious."

She swallowed.

"Driven... responsible... ambitious..." He cupped her chin with his palm.

The words that kept tumbling from his lips were ones she'd always associated with being dull, boring, or negative. Words people had thrown at her like she was somehow broken. But the way he said them, the way he stared at her made it sound like she was pretty fucking awesome.

"So accepting of people and so ready to fight for a cause." He threaded his fingers into the hair by her ear and tipped her head back just enough so their eyes met. "I need you to understand that I'm ready to fight for you and your causes, Q."

Her body vibrated, like she was a bottle of Coke and he'd dropped a Mentos in and screwed the lid tight.

If he knew the truth about her, about her past, would he still feel the same way?

She angled her face away, but he caught her with the knuckle of his index finger. "What is it?"

She swallowed again, chin trembling, lip quivering, and eyes filling. "I don't really talk to my family."

His brows knotted, lips pressed together in a grim line. "I figured. You don't ever really talk about your family, period." He led her to the couch, and she perched herself on the edge of one of the cushions while he sat next to her, taking her hands in his.

"Before you, I've only ever had one long-term boyfriend." Her palms were already damp, but it didn't seem to bother him, and no matter how desperate the urge to pull away, the need to be close to him shouted louder.

"I got pregnant at sixteen."

The creases between his brows deepened, but he didn't speak. Her skin crawled.

"From the second the lines appeared on the test I knew what I was going to do." She gave him a small smile as her insides churned. "I was barely past childhood myself. My parents' marriage was on the rocks. They were both always so busy... my Gramps took care of me more than they did. I wasn't ready to bring a child into the world."

She nibbled on her lip for a second before continuing. "My boyfriend at the time, the father... he pressured me to keep the baby, said he didn't want to murder our unborn child. He said we'd be a family together – he'd take care of me." She closed her eyes like that could protect her from the memories. Hot tears trickled down her cheeks.

"But I couldn't." She wouldn't defend her choice to Will. It was the right one for her at the time, and she couldn't bear the thought of him agreeing with her ex, so she just kept going. "So I made the appointment. I was working myself up to tell my parents..." Her voice dropped to barely a whisper, cracking with each word. "But he told them first."

Will's nostrils flared. His jaw twitched. But still, he didn't speak.

"I got home to find my stuff already packed by the door. Mom gave me an ultimatum. She told me I was either going to keep the baby or they were done with me."

His eyes flexed wide, but the silence continued.

"They stood and watched while I loaded my bags into the little beater Gramps gave me and drove away. I got to Gramps's house and told him everything, terrified he'd kick me out, too." She fidgeted with the corsage on her wrist. "He took me in, took me to my appointment, took care of me... he even paid for my college tuition."

The tears came faster. "He's gone now." She gnawed at her lip. "He left me everything he had in his will. Once I pay for college tuition..." She shrugged. "There isn't much left over.

But he saved me. From homelessness, from my parents... from myself."

She sucked in a shaky breath, wiping her cheeks with the heels of her hands. "I don't regret my decision. Not for a second. It was what I need—"

His thumb brushed over her lips. "You don't need to justify yourself. Not to me, not to anyone."

A wave of relief made her body deflate like a balloon. "I know you love kids. I do, too. And I want a family someday. But even though I don't regret my decision..." She rubbed at her breast bone. "Sometimes the guilt..." The words stuck in her throat.

He stood and offered his hand. Taking it, she let him help her to her feet. Cupping her face with both hands he swept his thumbs over her damp cheeks. "I love you, Quinn. All of you. And while I'm furious at your parents, and your ex, your past only serves to make me love you even harder. You have no idea how strong you are."

She tried to shake her head against his hands. "I don't always feel strong."

"That doesn't make it any less true."

Covering his hands with hers, she squeezed, laced her fingers into his, and led him to the bedroom. As she stood facing the bed, he slipped his hands around her waist and hugged her to his chest, kissing the bare skin of her shoulders. "We should have fundraisers every single week."

She rolled her head away from him, creating space as his feather light kisses made their way up the column of her neck.

"This is a good look for you."

"Not to sound like a broken record, buuuuuut... the penguin thing works for you, too, William."

He splayed a palm over her stomach, holding her in place while the other hand skimmed up her back to the zipper and swept her hair over her one shoulder. Dotting kisses along the back of her neck he eased the zipper down. "I've missed you, Q."

She jiggled her ass against his erection with a giggle. "Like I couldn't tell."

Spinning her to face him, he frowned. "Do you know how difficult it is to hide a hard on in dress pants? The answer is very. It's very hard. I have been in various states of painfully hard for you all damn night, Q."

He kept tugging the zipper, agonizingly slowly, their closeness cranking up her anticipation to almost intolerable levels. His smell, his soft touch, the way he handled her with such care... She inhaled deeply. "You smell so good."

When he'd fully opened the zip, the dress dropped from her chest, and she shimmied it down past her hips, enjoying the cool air and the feel of the satin as it skimmed over her skin.

He was already unbuckling his belt, shucking off his shoes and socks with his toes.

"You in a hurry?"

The only answer she got was a heated glare that made her reach out and tug open his tie. Her fingers worked over the buttons of his shirt until they both stood staring at each other in their underwear.

While she wasn't wearing shapewear, or – for that matter – her period panties, her nude strapless bra and matching underwear weren't exactly the sexiest things she owned. And yet, the way he was eye fucking her made her wonder.

She reached out and palmed his length through his boxer briefs, enjoying the way his head lolled back and his eyes fluttered closed at her touch. But as much as she wanted to savor every inch of him, it had been far too long since he'd been inside her.

Unhooking her bra, she let it fall to the floor on top of her dress, her panties followed suit before she stepped out of the pile of fabric, kicked off her heels, and climbed onto the bed.

"Now who's in a hurry?"

She held up a finger. "My patience is hanging by a thread, William. So I'm going to say this once, and once only. Get. Inside. Me. Now." She pointed to her crotch for good measure, in case he decided to wind her up.

Already stepping out of his undies, he grinned at her. "Why didn't you say so?"

He kissed her as he settled between her thighs, his hand caressing the length of her legs as they folded around his waist. "So soft."

"You can thank Bre for that later. I wasn't going to shave my legs."

He chuckled, rubbing his chin against the sensitive space where her shoulder joined her neck, making her shiver. "I wouldn't care if you didn't."

Brushing her slit with the tip of his cock, a shudder rippled through him. She tightened her legs around his waist, her arms around his neck, and kissed him harder, pressing her tongue against his to convey the fierce urgency roaring through her veins.

She needed him.

He inched inside her, excruciatingly slowly, hissing out a slow breath as her walls gripped him with fervor. "So tight."

She flexed her muscles around him, and his eyes rolled back in his head. "Careful, or our makeup sex will be over before it's even started, Q."

Arching her back, she tilted her pelvis to meet his, desperate for him to move, for any kind of friction, for him to sink deeper into her. She slid her hands down his back, grazing his skin with her nails, but when she got to his ass, she dug them into his cheeks and grunted. "Deeper. Stop teasing me."

His chest rumbled with a chuckle as she kissed him, gripping him against her, and he finally relented, giving her the last few inches of himself with such tenderness it almost brought her to tears.

She sagged against the bed, but didn't let him go. He pulled almost all the way out, sending a ripple through her protesting muscles before rutting back in without warning. She moaned, writhing underneath him, and pressed her nails deeper into his ass, but he held still again.

"William." His name was a growl.

He slipped his hand between them, and the pad of his thumb found her clit, making her breath catch. Her back arched further, and he took the opportunity to swirl his tongue around her nipple before scraping his teeth against the hard bud.

His hips moved, slowly at first, like his thumb, circling around the tight bundle of nerves that drove her closer and closer to insanity. The faster he drove into her, the louder her cries grew.

The edges of her vision blurred as her muscles tensed. He gritted his teeth before nipping at her jaw.

Every thrust of his hips, each circle of his thumb sent sparks to her bubbling climax. When his tongue met hers, her orgasm exploded at the base of her spine, sending shockwaves to every corner of her body. Wave after wave of undulating bliss coursed through her as he grunted, his movements becoming less rhythmic, more chaotic.

Gripping her hips, he came with a groan before whispering 'I love yous' against her skin as he kissed every inch of her body while she recovered.

It didn't take him long to reload, and before long, his hard cock pressed against her thigh. "Ready for round two?"

She paused for a moment, taking in the depths of his eyes, the angles of his jaw, his nose and his chestnut hair that fell over his forehead. She absorbed the warmth from his palms as he cradled her like she was a precious gem, the strength that reinforced her every cell when he looked at her like she could do anything she put her mind to, and the love that radiated from him.

She wasn't just ready for round two, she was ready for forever.

WILL

3 months later

It was weird sitting in the stands watching the Snow Pirates on the ice. And while they'd always be *his* Snow Pirates, they'd grown and changed, just like he had.

Finn elbowed him. "Getting nostalgic over there?"

"How'd you guess?"

Finn shrugged as some flyboy rookie on the Raccoons dropped his gloves at Linc's feet. "You got this far away look in your eyes."

On the ice, Linc quirked his brow at his opponent. He and Russ were seniors, Séb was a sophomore, and a bunch of fresh-faces he didn't recognize wore Snow Pirates shirts on the ice and on the bench.

Linc turned, skating away, but the kid didn't quit, chasing after him and pawing at his elbow like a puppy demanding attention.

Will shook his head, and Finn whistled. "That kid is playing with fire."

He leaned forward, elbows on his knees, waiting, watching, holding his breath and silently willing Linc to both skate away and clock the idiot to teach him a lesson.

Cooler heads prevailed. One of the rookie's teammates rescued him from a Lincoln Scott sized beat down, and Linc skated back to the bench.

The last few minutes of the third period ticked down, and Will couldn't wait to have a beer with his boys. It had been a long couple of weeks getting the bakery ready for Quinn's grand opening. Their friends had been instrumental in setting it up, and while Quinn had promised them all delicious opening day treats, Will had promised them beer.

By the time the team joined them in the bar, Finn was already on stage singing Toto's *Africa* at the top of his lungs. Every time he got to the chorus, he waved his hands at the crowd who were only too happy to join him with the uncomfortably high singing that got even louder at the *ooh oohs*.

Quinn flicked through the folder of songs like she wasn't going to choose the same ones she always did, while Kenzie pointed over her shoulder, nodding enthusiastically with each page turn.

Linc kissed Cleo at the bar, and Sabrina hugged Russell like she hadn't seen him in months.

Will had been going to therapy a few times a week for the past few months. While his demons still took up residence in a corner of his chest, he'd learned how to carry them with him better through his daily life.

Ms. Phillips had been brought up on charges as Will and a number of other young men stepped forward to tell their stories. It hadn't been easy, but with the strength and encouragement of his friends and family, he was going to be okay.

As he surveyed the smiling faces scattered around the bar, he realized they were all going to be okay.

The DJ called him to the stage, and Finn threw him a double thumbs up as he passed a gawping Quinn and Kenzie.

"Can he sing?" Kenzie didn't even try to hide her shock.

"I-I don't think so."

He'd make her pay for that later, but for the time being, he had something to say and he wasn't chickening out now. Why did people pick on chickens anyway? Like chickening out was something weak. Had they seen a chicken in action? Those suckers were vicious.

Tapping on the microphone, he cleared his throat. If possible, Quinn's jaw had dropped even further and her eyes were wide as she watched him.

"For those of you who don't already know, tomorrow morning marks the first day of my beautiful girlfriend's new adventure."

Quinn's face turned red to a chorus of whoops, hollers, and applause.

"*Cake My Day* opens bright and early at 9AM for business, and I couldn't be prouder. We are both truly grateful to our Snow Pirates family for stepping up and helping out over the past few months. We couldn't have done it without each and every one of you."

"Especially me." Finn raised his bottle into the air and Molly smacked his arm, but he wasn't wrong.

The DJ started the music and the words of Stevie Wonder's *I Just Called To Say I Love You* appeared on the screen. Finn jumped to his feet and rushed onto the stage, staying a foot away from Will as he started to sing.

"Just in case you need rescuing, man. I gotchu, boo."

Will clutched the microphone and sang at Quinn, who beamed up at him, her hands clasped in front of her chest as she mouthed every word, swaying to the music like he was Stevie Wonder himself. As Kenzie would say: Bless her heart.

Sabrina slinked onto a chair as Quinn checked out the last customer. Cleo swept the floor, and Molly typed on her laptop in the corner, slurping on an oversized cold brew.

As Quinn closed the door and flipped the *Open* sign to *Closed* she heaved out a deep breath.

"That was so intense." Molly raised her drink. "But you did great."

Cleo rolled her eyes. "Uh huh. You were so helpful over there, Molly."

"I am too helpful. I've been working her social media accounts all day. You should see her, she's all over the 'Gram."

"I am?" Quinn tucked the sweaty frizzy wisps behind her ear.

Molly grinned, nodding. "And Tiktok. I created an account for *Cake My Day* and we're already at over 500 followers."

Bre raised her hand. "I had a few customers say they saw us on Tiktok. But I thought someone bought a cupcake and shared it on their account."

"That could also have happened." Molly took another drink. "We make a great team."

She wasn't wrong. Will and Finn had left an hour ago to get ready for the First Mate's game. But for the help of their friends, Quinn would have been screwed on her opening day.

She'd almost cleared out of everything she'd baked and her feet hurt, but her heart was happy.

Nova peered around the *closed* sign in the window, knocking on the glass. "Let me in, Quinn. I come bearing booze." She held up a dark bottle by its neck and rapped the glass again.

When Quinn opened the door, Nova burst in with Pippa hot on her heels. Pippa handed out plastic cups while Nova jammed the champagne bottle between her thighs and twisted the cage over the cork.

Molly tapped some keys on her laptop and *Word Up* by Cameo started playing around the room. She dragged Sabrina to her feet and started dancing.

Champagne in hand, butts swaying to the music, Molly lifted her Solo cup high in the air. "Ladies, join me in a toast. To the best cupcake maker and future sister-in-law in Minnesota, on chasing down her dreams like the badass bish she is."

While they toasted her, Quinn's mouth dried up. Sister-in-law? Sure, she wanted to be with Will forever, but the mention of forever from someone other than her or Will, made her freeze in place.

Bre wrapped her arms around Quinn. "I'm so proud of you, Quinny."

For the first time in a long time she was proud of herself, too. Pippa squeezed her biceps, a wide grin on her face. "I'm proud of you too, kiddo."

She rolled her eyes at the word kiddo, but Pippa's words warmed something inside her chest. "Thank you."

"You know my birthday's coming up, right?"

She nodded.

"I'm gonna need some cock-cakes."

She was in bed reading when Will got home from the game. When he entered the room, he already had his shirt balled in his hand and was unbuttoning his pants. "Enjoying the view?"

She licked her top lip. "Always."

"Wanna join me in the shower?"

Flinging back the quilt with one hand, she rose from the bed, tucked a bookmark between the pages, and placed the book on her bedside cabinet.

Will gave a low whistle as she rounded the foot of the bed. Slipping his finger under the strap of her lacy camisole, a grumble rolled around his chest. "Moving in together was the best idea I've ever had."

She popped him on the nose with the tip of her finger. "You mean it's the best idea Russell ever had, right?"

Russ had asked Sabrina to move in with him and Jude when their lease ran out. Instead of renewing the lease and finding a new roommate, Russ had alluded to the idea that Quinn could move in with Will to save the hassle. Considering how much time they spent together, it was a no brainer for both of them.

He slid the straps from her shoulder and tugged the hem of the nightdress until it gave away and fell to the floor before toeing off his pants and undies. Cupping her ass cheeks, he picked her up, wrapping her legs around his waist and sliding his hands up her back, sending goosebumps all over her body.

"What a day..." She tipped her head back for him to kiss her neck. "Wait. Did the First Mates win?"

He paused, giving her a look like she'd lost her goddamn

mind, and stepped into the bathroom. Holding her with one arm as she clung to him like a koala, he flipped the shower on to warm up the water.

"You taste of strawberries and champagne." Will kissed her again, deeper, his stiff cock pressing into the apex of her thighs.

Dotting kisses along his jaw, she nodded. "Nova brought champagne and we had some strawberry cupcakes leftover."

He pressed her back against the cold tiled wall and kissed her. His hands gripped her tightly and his tongue searched her mouth like he owned it. Pulling back, a frown knotted his forehead.

"What?"

"Marry me." He shook his head. "Not right now. But—"

She was already nodding. "Okay."

"Okay?"

She nodded again.

His frown deepened. Her stomach fell.

Didn't he mean it?

"I... I hadn't planned to ask like this." He tipped his chin at their naked bodies. "I don't even have a ring." He groaned and dropped his forehead to hers. "Mom is gonna *kill* me."

She giggled. "Can we not talk about your mom while your cock is pressed against my pussy please?"

He nodded. "You'll really marry me?"

"If you really meant to ask me." She stroked the soft tufts of hair at the nape of his neck, twisting the longer strands around her fingers.

When his eyes met hers, his sincerity punched her in the chest, sucking the oxygen from her lungs.

"I meant it with everything I am, Q. I want you to be my wife."

She tightened her grip around his neck. "Then my answer

stands. I'd be honored to be your wife, William. I've been ready for forever for a while."

If you'd like to read more about Will and Quinn, you can find their bonus epilogue here.

Read on to get a sneak peek of Coach Elliott's book, Two for Charging, now!

CHAPTER 21

Clare

"Regular flow or heavy?" Clare pursed her lips and regarded the selection of care products in front of her. "What a total crock of shit."

No matter how bright and attractive companies made the packaging, a period still felt like a sucker punch to the uterus.

By a bear.

With a fucking jackhammer.

There was no way to make that shit cute. Period products *lied.* No one was that chipper when Aunt Flo came to visit. And if they were, they were probably a serial killer... Because they had their fucking period.

If they offered a "swamp witch" variety of Tampax, however, she'd hand them her PIN number in a flash. A haggard woman shoveling a gallon of ice cream into her pimpletastic face while crying over every teeny tiny little thing and shitting through the eye of a goddamn needle. Period poop was no fucking joke.

She swiped a packet from the shelf and waved it high above her head. "Cat? Regular or heavy?"

Silence. Her nineteen-year-old daughter was nowhere to

be seen. Maybe she'd gone back out to the car. Or maybe she was hiding behind a display of Lindor chocolate balls, pretending she was in no way related to the wild woman muttering to herself about periods and pads.

Fine. If her dearest darling daughter was embarrassed by her, she'd double down. She grabbed one of each, regular, heavy, and overnight pads, and snagged regular and heavy tampons for good measure.

Humming *Sisters Are Doin' it for Themselves* by Eurythmics, she inched toward the end of the aisle.

The benefit of having the Leaning Tower of Period Products stacked high in her arms was that she couldn't reach the shelf of Lindor balls. Or carry any chocolate at all for that matter. A fact her fast tightening jeans would thank her for.

She'd let herself go since the divorce. She wasn't one of those women who'd caught her husband cheating on her and used it to drop twenty pounds and fuel some rage-filled magic makeover.

The only thing it had fueled was depression, self-loathing, and a need to buy bigger pants. And the only thing she'd dropped was her self-respect.

"Asshole." She glared at the Lindor chocolate like it was the one who had banged their secretary on the family dining table and not her piece-of-shit ex.

Rounding the end of the aisle, she crashed into something, her body tensing as the collision knocked the air out of her. The pads and tampons flew from her arms like someone had pulled out a wooden Jenga block from her carefully crafted and precariously balanced tower.

"Oof! Sorry." Her muttered apology was aimed at the sneakers of the person she'd bumped into as she bent over to pick up her fallen spoils with a weighty sigh.

That's what she got for trying to embarrass her daughter. Apparently Karma worked fast when it was against her. If only it would work as quickly on her ex—maybe give him a raging case of crabs, or remove all the labels from the cans of food in his pantry.

Ha! If only.

The body in front of her didn't move, so she abandoned the period product recovery plan in favor of shooing off the person looming over her. She'd said sorry, what else could Mr. Bootcut Jeans want?

As she straightened, the back of her head connected with something hard and she winced. Pain rippled across her scalp. She hadn't even planned on stopping at CVS on her way home, but Catriona was desperate and now it was a thing.

But based on how the pharmacy was going, dinner would be drive-thru Panera. Relatively healthy and minimal people-ing. If the car found its way into the drive-thru at Taco Bell, she wouldn't be mad about it.

"Sorry. Here. Let me." A gravelly voice that sent tingles all the way to her toes instantly cured her brewing concussion. A firm grip banded around her bicep, helping her straighten up. All the oxygen evaporated from her body.

"Elliott." His name caught in her throat, croaking like it had been trapped there for decades. It kind of had.

The boy she'd once loved was all man now. Square jaw covered with a neat, dark, salt-and-pepper beard that her fingers itched to reach out and stroke. Small crow's feet crin-kling the corners of his eyes. Brown, wavy hair, still styled with gel but with a dusting of gray at the temples.

He'd aged well. Too well.

Clare knew those hazel eyes. She'd stared into them when she'd pressed a sweater against his face after he'd taken a stray puck to the eyebrow in a game of street hockey when he was a kid. She'd stared at them over numerous games of cribbage in her backyard. It had taken her a while to get used to the card game with the little peg stand, but once she'd mastered counting points in combinations of fifteens, it was on like *Donkey Kong*.

She'd pleaded with them when he'd told her he was going to be leaving and pursuing his dreams. Those hazel eyes were burned into her memory forever.

She'd heard he was coaching the local college hockey team. Sure, he had a little squish around his middle underneath his solid black t-shirt—probably from moving into coaching rather than still playing—but he was still every bit Elliott.

Her Elliott.

She swallowed down the bitter taste in her mouth. He wasn't hers anymore. Perhaps he never had been.

He'd done good things with the team, great, in fact. If she wasn't still pissed at him she'd be proud of him. Her heart twisted. She was always proud of him.

She smoothed her hand over her not-been-washed-in-a-week hair, face aflame, and gave an awkward laugh. "Elliott."

Why did her voice sound so... weird?

His eyebrows were arched high. His jaw hung open. The golden-brown circle around the pupil in his left eye caught the light as his gaze bore into hers, as though searching for something. Mute.

Silently urging him to speak, she slid her damp palms over the thighs of her yoga pants. Had she let herself go so much that he didn't even recognize her? Or was he simply stunned at the fact she was wearing yesterday's *Feminist AF* shirt?

Okay, so her toothpaste had splattered on it a bit, but it kind of looked like it was supposed to be that way, so she'd just gone with it. Another tuck of her hair behind her ear, another awkward giggle.

"Okay. Um." She gestured at the boxes and packets on the ground and crouched to pick them up, careful to avoid another collision against...well...any part of him.

As though her bending snapped him out of whatever daze

he was in, he squatted in front of her, scrambling to pick up the boxes.

Definitely Karma. His thighs filled out his jeans like he'd been poured into the denim. Was it weird to want to bite someone's thigh? She wasn't sure she cared.

His eyes were still on her when they stood again. He offered her the heavy flow and overnight pads with a raised eyebrow. His lips twitched like he fought a smile.

Her face was on fire. No, she wasn't lucky enough to be on fire. But the heat of her cheeks could most definitely have started one. "They're for my daughter."

Fan-fucking-tastic. Now he probably thought her daughter was having some kind of severe period emergency that required almost forty pads and the same number of tampons.

Closing her eyes for a beat, Clare sucked in an audible breath through her nose. Maybe if she didn't meet his confused, amused, and bottomless gaze she'd be able to jump-start her brain with the heat radiating from the rest of her body.

If only wishing made it so.

When she opened her eyes, he was still there, head canted, smile teasing at the corners of his lips. She pinned her stare to the center of his chest, but couldn't make her feet move away from him.

He was still voiceless, and she was stuck. Two decades ago they'd have dissolved into a fit of laughter over the whole thing. But now? Their history stretched out between them like taffy in summer heat in the heavy silence.

Too much history. Too much time.

Swallowing down the lump forming in her throat, she turned toward the counter and strode away with purpose. Every fiber of her being wanted to abandon Operation Shark Week and flee the state, but Catriona needed provisions. Plus, if she ran, he'd totally know she was rattled.

Hell, he probably already knew. He always had known her better than she even knew herself. But she wasn't going to let him see it. Forcing a smile for the cashier, she paid for her items and waved off the receipt. Who needed to take proof of the dreaded *pink tax* home with them?

Who needed to carry around a record of such an inordinate spend on something that cost mere pennies to make? Especially for shit that damn near every woman of a certain age needed.

Was she deflecting the fact Elliott's burning gaze still pierced her back at the checkout with ire at Proctor and Gamble? Maybe.

Did she pick up a packet of gum, two Snickers, and a bag of Sour Patch Kids for a second transaction to buy time so she could pull her shit together before turning to face him again? Damn straight she did.

Hopefully if she took long enough at the checkout, when she turned around, he'd magically be gone. A hallucination. A figment of her imagination conjured to remind her that despite being screwed over by her asshole ex, she was still a woman, still had needs. She was divorced for crying out loud, not dead.

He cleared his throat as she declined the second receipt. No such luck. She shoved the candy into her mom-bag. Either she'd find them again in a month or two in a moment of dire snack-emergency, or Catriona would find them and remove the temptation when she next *borrowed* twenty bucks.

She thanked the cashier with a tight-lipped smile.

The young woman, whose name tag was hidden by her jacket, leaned forward, jerking her chin at Elliott, and lowered her voice. "Ma'am, is that guy bothering you?"

Clare snorted, almost choking on her own tongue, but

shook her head. "No, we're old friends. Thanks for looking out for me though."

The young woman didn't seem convinced, but she nodded. "We get some weirdos around here sometimes."

Was she calling Elliott the weirdo, or her? Either way, she wasn't wrong.

"Clare?"

She spun to face him. "Elliott." Yup. She'd said nothing but his name to him, three times and counting. While she might have enjoyed how her tongue felt around it, he probably already knew his own name.

An uncertain smile spread across his face as he opened his arms. Was he going to hug her? Cheese and crackers, hell no. If he did that, she'd be forced to feel him all around her, and she might do something even more embarrassing than covering him in boxes of Tampax...like...sniff him. Did he still smell of soap?

She held up her two bags as though they were enough of an explanation as to why she couldn't return his hug.

"Long time." His sad eyes almost made her want to drop her bags and throw herself into his arms.

Almost.

"Yeah. Long time." It was the understatement of the century, but she nodded.

"How are you? You look good."

And he was still a lying liar who lied. He told her he wouldn't leave to play hockey. And when he did, he told her he'd come back. He never came back.

A zebra never changed its stripes. Or whatever the hell the thing about people never changing was. Clearly his presence still fucked up her ability to think straight.

"You too."

He tucked his hands into his back pockets and rocked

back on his heels like an *aw shucks* teenager asking a girl out for the first time.

She almost laughed. "Well, I better get going." She lifted her bags again. Another reminder of the Big Red Emergency. Peachy.

All she needed to do to complete her mortification, was to trip over thin air and land on her face as she left.

"Clare?"

She was almost at the door before that voice crashed into her again, stopping her in her tracks and warming her all over.

That was her name, don't wear it out. Pausing, she turned her chin over her shoulder, but he didn't say anything else. She turned a little more, enough to see his brows knit into a frown and a huge sigh escape him.

He tossed her a half-shrug. "It was good to see you."

Liar. A pap smear would have been more enjoyable, and he didn't even have a fucking cervix. Rolling her lips between her teeth in a bid to stop a salty response from breaking free, she nodded. "You too."

She sank into the driver's seat of her car and tossed the bag over her shoulder into the back seat. Then she slammed the door. She wouldn't cry. She wouldn't look at the door to CVS because he'd undoubtedly be standing there, watching her hot mess self having a nervous breakdown at seeing him.

She was pulling out of the parking lot when movement in the rearview mirror caught her attention. Catriona stood at the entrance to the drugstore, waving both her hands like she was stranded at sea and flagging down a rescue.

Clare slammed on the brakes. She'd forgotten her fucking daughter. Though the way the kid stood swinging her hands over her head was testament to the fact she had indeed been hiding inside the building and ignoring Clare's hollering outright.

Jerking the door to the passenger seat open, Catriona

erupted into a fit of giggles. "I can't believe you were going to drive off without me, Mom."

"And I can't believe you hid in the drugstore and pretended I wasn't asking you questions about your period products."

The mother of all eye rolls preceded a tut. "I can't believe you were asking me questions about my period products in a voice that was not what anyone would have considered a suitable indoor voice."

It was her turn to eye roll. There was no mistaking where her kid got her sassitude from.

"Know what else I can't believe, Mom?"

Clare quirked her brow as she pulled out of the parking lot for the second time.

"I can't believe you're just driving home as though we're going to ignore the fact you were just talking to a hottie in the drugstore. Well." She held up a palm before another fit of giggles hit. "I don't think we could really call that talking, can we?"

Clare groaned. They were not having that conversation. "I need to concentrate on the road."

"Right. That would be a first." An indignant snort rang from her kid as the light at the intersection changed to red.

"Shit."

"Nice try. You don't need to concentrate on the road when we're sitting still, do you, Mom? Spill. Tell me *everything* about the hunky silver fox makin' eyes at you over tampons at the store."

Silver fox? They weren't that old, were they? Dear Jesus in the manger, please tell her they weren't at silver fox age quite yet.

"He's just someone I used to know." Her fingers tapped on the steering wheel as her glare bored into the red light hanging in front of her.

"How?" Catriona tore open a box of Whoppers and dropped a couple into her mouth.

"School." The traitorous light was still red, and a sidelong glance at Cat told her the conversation was far from over.

"Which one?" Another Whopper down the hatch. Cat seemed to have inherited her father's metabolism. She could eat cosmic crap tons of whatever the hell she wanted and she didn't gain an ounce. Bitch. "High school?"

Clare shook her head. Still red.

"College?"

Another head shake. If a kangaroo could hop across the intersection to change the topic of conversation from Elliott fucking Swift that would be great. Perhaps answering the question and giving her something, anything to mull over, would shut up the inquisition.

"Kindergarten." There. She'd given her something to chew on. It wasn't exactly a salacious detail, but it was something.

Cat coughed, choking on a piece of candy, and thumped her chest a few times. "You've known him since you were little and you still acted like..." She waved her hand as though that was enough of an explanation of her behavior. She wasn't wrong.

Mercifully, the light changed to green, Clare let her foot off the brake, and a silence descended over the car. "Yeah."

After a few minutes Cat leaned forward and turned the radio on. "Mom?"

"Yeah?"

"What's his name?"

"Elliott."

"I gave him your number."

Continue Elliott and Clare's story now!

When I was eleven years old, I managed to convince my parents to let me go on a school trip away from home. It was a few days, almost two hundred miles from home, and there wasn't a parent in sight.

We stayed in a youth hostel and – long story short – before long, it became apparent to a few of us that one of the members of staff was just a liiiiittle too friendly with the kids who were staying there. He kissed one of them on the forehead, got a bit handsy with a few others (myself included), he followed one or two to the bathroom, and one night I even woke up to him sitting on the end of my bed watching me sleep.

We were terrified. We wound up doubling up in our bunkbeds so we wouldn't be sleeping alone. When we told the teachers what was happening they told us not to tell our parents, they'd talk to the manager of the hostel and 'handle things'.

Knowing the difference between right and wrong, and knowing my parents would be mad if I *didn't* tell them, I called them and told them what was going on. My dad called the local police department and by the time they got to the hostel the guy was gone.

The teachers talked to the managing staff, who likely tipped off/scared off the employee, and the guy disappeared into the wind.

Despite the fact the man touched me over my clothes and didn't assault me 'all that bad' it impacted me on a deep level. I'd been sheltered by my parents, I didn't have my first boyfriend until I was a few years older, and the idea that a grown up could touch a child inappropriately like that broke something inside of me.

I had nightmares for months. I woke up screaming in a wet bed with my dad holding me and telling me everything was going to be okay. I had friends who were on the trip tell me it wasn't a big deal, that it didn't even count as sexual assault, and with teachers telling me not to tell my parents it was made to feel like some huge overreaction on my part.

It's something I carried with me for a long time: I was just being dramatic. It wasn't a big deal. I must have done *something* to make the man think it was okay to smack my ass and feel me up the way he did. I must have been wrong to question the teachers when they said not to tell our parents.

I... I... I...

Everything was my fault, and I never once thought of myself as the victim.

And yet, I was an eleven year old child – nothing I said, did, or should have, or could have said or done differently gave anyone the right to touch my body. As grown-ups, my teachers were entrusted with my safety and they should have informed parents and acted in the best interests of us – the victims – from the moment we told them what was going on.

When I started digging into Will as a character, I was every bit as taken aback and confused by his intense slut shaming of his sister. And as the author, I started to panic. Will was such a nice guy for the most part, sweet, caring, a great leader, someone his team could depend on at all times... but the slut shaming. Damn.

I know for so many people – almost myself included – there's no coming back from that. And I'd feared I'd written an irredeemable hero. But the more he and I talked – yes, I talk to my characters – the more he let me inside his world and I realized that his reactions came from a place of pain.

I don't talk about my childhood experience very often. I guess part of me still feels like I still somehow overreacted to it, and on some level, maybe I even believe it was my own fault, or I somehow deserved it.

But I wanted to address it with Will. I wanted to face it head on and confront it. I wanted to shine a light on male sexual assault. And I wanted to remind people that you have no fucking clue what's going on in anyone's lives.

It wasn't an easy book to write, it wasn't smooth sailing by any means. Digging up those pieces of my past were difficult. I remember my parents taking the teachers to court for negligence. I remember how I was supposed to have a closed session with just the judge, but at the last minute it was changed to an open session. This meant the teachers who were on the trip would sit there and watch me tell my story and I couldn't do it.

I broke down outside the courtroom and cried hysterically to my parents and our lawyer, pleading with them not to make me go in and tell my story in front of all those people. The shame and embarrassment was real. The fear was real. The self-doubt was real. Going into that courtroom and telling my story would have had a terrible impact on the grownups lives and I was scared to damage their reputations, even though I was right.

Writing through Will's eyes reminded me of that time. It made me grateful for having supportive parents who went to bat for me so damn hard when I told them what happened. They never once made me feel like it was in any way my fault, or that I was overreacting, or that I could have somehow prevented it.

For those of you who know my work, you know I put pieces of myself in each of my books. This book was a painful piece, a piece that hurts me to talk about, it hurts to relive, and it hurts to put out there. But I know it's necessary. I know it's important. I know that through Will's story, this book might somehow help other people who went through similar experiences to Will and me. And that's why it's all worthwhile.

For those of you who might need support with the issues mentioned in this book, here are some resources you might find useful:

US:

RAINN (Rape, Abuse & Incest National Network.) www.rainn.org

National Sexual Violence Resource Center www.nsvrc.org

UK:

Survivors UK (for men and non-binary people who have been affected by rape or sexual abuse.) www.survivorsuk.org

Rape Crisis England and Wales Freephone 0808 802 9999

Rape Crisis Northern Ireland https://rapecrisisni.org.uk/

Acknowledgments

Lewis – My darling wee man. You're only eight years old, yet every book I write is – in some part – down to you. With this one, I set a goal. A big monthly word goal. We broke out the Post It notes a-la-Nanowrimo and got shit done. You pushed me hard, and with each Post It you ticked off the mirror, you cheered harder. I love you most, kiddo.

Tracie and Clare – My sprint bitches, my work wives, and two of the most talented people I know. Thank you for being there for me every morning for 6am sprints, without you, I'd succumb to the lure of procrastination, to the depths of impostor syndrome, and my life wouldn't be as rich.

Heather – I'm never one to take my friends for granted, so it's important to me to mention just how much you mean to me in my acknowledgements – just in case you forget. Thanks for being my chosen family, and stepping up when I feel like I'm completely alone and overwhelmed. I appreciate you.

My parents – If you've been in my life for any length of time you'll know I don't have the best relationship with my family. My father passed away in November 2019 and I haven't spoken to my siblings or my mother since.

That said, when it comes to this book and these themes, I probably wouldn't have been able to write something so close to home if it hadn't been for their love and support in getting me through this experience as a kid.

They were fierce advocates of me when I told them about what happened on my school trip. They rallied around me, sat with me until long after I fell asleep, and helped get me through an experience that left scars on my life.

I know other victims don't get the level of support I had, I know how lucky I am, and even though they aren't around anymore, it's important for me to mention that I appreciate them being stellar parents for me during a horrible time. I'm so grateful.

My Alphas – Savannah, Amy R, Erika, Robynne and **My Betas** – Micky and Corinne. I can cause terrible ball ache with my self-doubts and whining at various points during my writing process. I know this. I do. It's a terrible affliction and no matter how many books I write, you're all basically screwed 'cause it never goes away. But that doesn't mean I don't appreciate y'all. Every head pat, every 'you got this,' every single time you read a book for me – whether you find typos, inconsistencies, or you just squee with delight, I appreciate it all. For realz. Thank you. And Shani – thank you for help with my dedication.

HUGE thanks to my editor Jami Nord and my cover designer Kate Farlow over at Y'all That Graphic.

And finally, to my ARC readers, my Facebook reader group *Margaritas, Men, and Mischief with Lasairiona*, and to each and every one of you who pick up this book: a bazillion thank yous. I truly hope you loved it enough to pick up the next one.

About the Author

Lasairiona McMaster writes sassy, classy and badassy women and strong, yet vulnerable men. She challenges reader's expectations by openly dealing with mental health issues, often exploring tough-to-handle topics and 'taboos' and books with a whole lotta heart.

She can either be found enjoying a gin and lemonade by the Irish sea, or baking sweet treats in her kitchen while singing at the top of her lungs. When she's 'home' in Texas, and isn't eating fresh-popped popcorn while buying things she has absolutely no need for in Target, she can be found at Chuys eating her body weight in chips and queso and washing it down with a margarita swirl. She loves to make friends out of strangers.

9 781913 878375